"Is this a ... Suzanne ...

"Yes," Grammy said. "I want you to take yours home with you today."

"But there's really no need. I'm not even dating anyone."

"Your love life will change soon," Grammy said with a wink. "Take a look through it."

Even though her cousins and sister claimed their hope chests had some kind of magical power that had given them hints as to their future husbands, Suzanne didn't believe it. She worked with facts and figures, not superstitions.

Suzanne opened the wooden chest and pushed aside layers of gold tissue paper, unearthing a white lacy Stetson, a pair of white Western lace-up boots and a lace ribbon choker.

Suzanne laughed outright. Grammy must have made a mistake when she'd put these things inside. Perhaps she'd meant them for someone else. Suzanne was a city girl. High heels and plunging necklines were more her style.

In fact, she'd use the choker to strangle herself before she'd marry someone who wanted a cowgirl bride. Wouldn't she?

Dear Reader,

This month Harlequin American Romance delivers favorite authors and irresistible stories of heart, home and happiness that are sure to leave you smiling.

COWBOYS BY THE DOZEN, Tina Leonard's new family-connected miniseries, premieres this month with *Frisco Joe's Fiancée*, in which a single mother and her daughter give a hard-riding, heartbreaking cowboy second thoughts about bachelorhood.

Next, in *Prognosis: A Baby? Maybe*, the latest book in Jacqueline Diamond's THE BABIES OF DOCTORS CIRCLE miniseries, a playboy doctor's paternal instincts and suspicions are aroused when he sees a baby girl with the woman who had shared a night of passion with him. Was this child his? THE HARTWELL HOPE CHESTS, Rita Herron's delightful series, resumes with *Have Cowboy, Need Cupid*, in which a city girl suddenly starts dreaming about a cowboy groom after opening an heirloom hope chest. And rounding out the month is *Montana Daddy*, a reunion romance and secret baby story by Charlotte Maclay.

Enjoy this month's offerings as Harlequin American Romance continues to celebrate its yearlong twentieth anniversary.

Melissa Jeglinski
Associate Senior Editor
Harlequin American Romance

HAVE COWBOY, NEED CUPID

Rita Herron

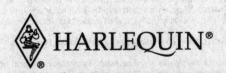

TORONTO • NEW YORK • LONDON
AMSTERDAM • PARIS • SYDNEY • HAMBURG
STOCKHOLM • ATHENS • TOKYO • MILAN • MADRID
PRAGUE • WARSAW • BUDAPEST • AUCKLAND

To my mother for teaching me to love country music
and my sister for making me appreciate a cowboy.

Also, to Paige & Scott for inspiring the cowboy wedding
with their own real one.

ISBN 0-373-16979-5

HAVE COWBOY, NEED CUPID

Visit us at www.eHarlequin.com

Printed in U.S.A.

ABOUT THE AUTHOR

Award-winning author Rita Herron wrote her first book when she was twelve, but didn't think real people grew up to be writers. Now she writes so she doesn't have to get a *real* job. A former kindergarten teacher and workshop leader, she traded her storytelling for kids for romance, and writes romantic comedies and romantic suspense. She lives in Georgia with her own romantic hero and three kids. She loves to hear from readers so please write her at P.O. Box 921225, Norcross, GA 30092-1225 or visit her Web site at www.ritaherron.com.

Books by Rita Herron

HARLEQUIN AMERICAN ROMANCE
820—HIS-AND-HERS TWINS
859—HAVE GOWN, NEED GROOM*
872—HAVE BABY, NEED BEAU*
883—HAVE HUSBAND, NEED HONEYMOON*
944—THE RANCHER WORE SUITS
975—HAVE BOUQUET, NEED BOYFRIEND*
979—HAVE COWBOY, NEED CUPID*

*The Hartwell Hope Chests

HARLEQUIN INTRIGUE
486—SEND ME A HERO
523—HER EYEWITNESS
556—FORGOTTEN LULLABY
601—SAVING HIS SON
660—SILENT SURRENDER†
689—MEMORIES OF MEGAN†
710—THE CRADLE MISSION†

†Nighthawk Island

Dear Suzanne,

You are a very special granddaughter because you go after what you want in life. When someone tells you no, you fight that much harder. And if you see someone in need, you are always there to encourage them to achieve their dreams.

You were the youngest of the family, the last symbol of your mother and father's love. You were the baby, but unfortunately you weren't babied for very long. When your mother died, you had to grow up fast. Your father thought his heart had been ripped out, but it ticked strongly inside you. You became his strength when he thought he had none left. You added a much-needed spark of joy to the quiet household, and you showed us all that even through grief and sadness, we must still strive for life.

But you never let yourself cry. You built an invisible wall, a tough veneer that sometimes keeps others from entering the closed doors to your heart. Sometimes, my dear, we have to tear down walls and clean out the cluttered attic to move forward. Sometimes we have to cry before we can free our souls to find that one perfect soul mate.

I wish for you happiness, true love and a man who can give you all the joy that a partner can.

Love you always,
Grammy Rose

P.S. Inside the hope chest you will find something old, something new, something borrowed and something blue.

Prologue

Rebecca tossed her bridal bouquet straight at Suzanne, but Suzanne jumped aside so she wouldn't catch it. So, how did it land in her hands anyway?

And why did she have this odd pang in her chest? This twinge of sadness.. Of envy. A feeling of desperation, as if she would never find a man who would look at her with adoration and unbridled passion in his eyes the way Thomas did Rebecca. Or the way her other cousins' husbands looked at them.

Maybe because your latest boyfriend just dumped you like the rest of the guys you dated.

Why did all those men keep dumping her? Did she have some big sign emblazoned on her forehead that said, Can't Love This One?

Sure, she knew how to attract a man, to cast the line and throw out the bait. A little flirting here. A smile there. Throw in some hip movement, and voilà, they chased her like flies after honey. But once they sampled a taste of the nectar, she never could quite keep them for more than a few quick bites.

The wedding drowned out her thoughts as everyone rushed past the white folding chairs, food-laden tables and the gazebo to see the bride and groom off on their honeymoon. The scent of freshly cut grass and wildflowers seemed to warm the cool air, the first signs of spring evident in the tulip bulbs sprouting along the mountaintop. Fading sunshine dappled golden rays over the happy couple as they stopped to laugh at the words Just Married painted on the back of Thomas's Porsche. Then Thomas folded Rebecca into his arms and kissed her, stirring a round of cheers and applause, and another bout of heartsickness rippled through Suzanne.

Drat. She did not need a man to be happy. She was managing fine on her own. Right?

"Have fun on your honeymoon!" Mimi shouted.

"Take lots of pictures," Alison yelled.

"Be happy," Grammy Rose hollered.

"Drive safely!" Hannah called.

Laughing and waving, Rebecca and Thomas climbed in his Porsche convertible, streamers and tin cans trailing behind the car compliments of her uncle Wiley.

Suzanne's father, Bert, strode up beside her, his ruddy face even pinker from emotions. A rarity for her father since his life normally revolved around work and making money. "That boy better take good care of Rebecca," her father said.

Suzanne tucked her hand in her father's bent arm. "I'm sure he will, Dad. They look totally in love."

Her father angled his head to study her. "What about you, baby? Are you happy?"

Suzanne frowned, surprised by her father's question. He usually didn't venture anywhere near such personal territory. "Of course," Suzanne replied automatically. She had a great job, a great condo, everything she wanted. Didn't she?

She stroked the delicate gold cross tucked between her breasts, the one her mother had given her before she'd died. "Always wear this and feel my love," her mother had whispered.

Suzanne had felt her love then, but she'd been angry that her mother was leaving her. Had she felt loved by anyone since? Sure, Rebecca loved her, and so did her father, but a man?

"Anyone special in your life?" her father asked, glancing at the bouquet. "A boyfriend I don't know about?"

"Dad, well…no, not now." Suzanne coughed nervously.

His graying eyebrow rose a fraction. "How about your boss?"

"James?"

"Yes, you and Horton seem to get along pretty well."

Suzanne frowned. "We work well together, but that's all there is to our relationship."

Her father's newest wife, Eleanor, coasted toward them, pearls dripping from her earlobes and neck, her pale-blue silk dress shimmering in the orange glow of the sunset. "Not everyone finds the romantic kind of love, Suzanne. But that doesn't mean you can't have a good partnership." He sipped his champagne. "You're a smart girl. You're going places in this world. Just keep that in mind and find someone who'll help you achieve your goals."

Her father kissed her goodbye, then curled his arm around Eleanor and headed toward her grandmother. Suzanne watched carefully, just in case he crossed paths with her uncle Wiley and the two of them got into one of their brotherly arguments. Although her father had promised to behave himself and not spoil Rebecca's wedding, Suzanne had become his self-appointed guard dog.

Her mission was accomplished when she saw him veer toward his Mercedes. Suzanne's gaze dropped to the bouquet in her hands, one finger tracing the edge of a delicate rose petal as she sniffed the heavenly fragrance. Maybe her father was right. Maybe she should consider the fact that she might not have a soul mate.

A few minutes later, when the crowd had dispersed, Suzanne found her grandmother in the homey kitchen. "I'm leaving now, Gram."

"Come into the parlor first, dear," Grammy Rose said.

Suzanne's stomach flip flopped. "Is this about the hope chest?" Rebecca and her cousins had already warned her.

"Yes, I want you to take yours home today."

"But, Grammy, there's really no need. I'm not even dating anyone." Suzanne followed her grandmother into the nostalgic parlor filled with antiques, silver-framed photos of family members and scrapbooks overflowing with memorabilia marking the special days in her grandchildren's lives. For some reason this room always brought a surge of emotions—feelings both happy and sad at the same time. Maybe it was the reason she'd opted for such modern decor in her own apartment. No frou-frou or sentiment...

"Your love life will change soon," Grammy said with a wink. "Now, I'm going to clean up in the kitchen if you want to look through the hope chest before you go."

Suzanne gulped, the telltale twinkle in her grandmother's eyes hinting that she was up to something. But even though her cousins and Rebecca claimed their hope chests had some kind of magical power that had hinted at their future husbands, Suzanne did not believe any of the nonsense. She worked with facts, figures and business deals, not superstitions or aphorisms. In fact, she would open the chest and look inside just to dispel her grandmother's romantic notions.

The ornately carved heart etched in the fine-grain wood was beautiful, she admitted, as was the fine gold latch and the soft burgundy velvet inside. Still, trepidation filled her as Suzanne pushed aside the layers of gold tissue paper. A small white envelope lay on top, trimmed with roses. She thumbed the seal open and unfolded a piece of lilac-scented stationery, her grandmother's loopy handwriting scrawled across the page.

Dear Suzanne,
You are a very special granddaughter because you go after what you want in life. When someone tells you no, you fight that much harder.

And if you see someone in need, you always encourage them to achieve their dreams.

You were the youngest of the family, the last legacy of your mother and father, the last symbol of their love. You were the baby, Suzanne, but unfortunately you weren't babied for very long. When your mother died, you had to grow up fast. Your father thought his heart had been ripped out, but it ticked strong and determined inside you. You became his strength when he thought he had none left. You added a much-needed spark of joy to the empty, quiet household, and you showed us all that even through grief and sadness, we must still strive for life.

But in your own sadness, you never let yourself cry. You built an invisible wall, a tough veneer that sometimes keeps others from entering the closed doors to your heart, from truly seeing inside. Sometimes, my dear, we have to tear down walls and clean out the cluttered attic to move forward. Sometimes we have to cry before we can free our souls to find that one perfect soul mate.

I wish for you happiness, true love and a man

who can give you all the joy that a partner can.
Love you always,
Grammy Rose

P.S. Inside the hope chest you will find something old, something new, something borrowed and something blue.

Suzanne blinked, a heaviness lodging in her throat. Good heavens alive, she was not the weepy type like Rebecca. She cried over TV commercials, but Suzanne *never* cried. Not even when her mother had died....

No, she'd had to be tough. And she always would be. Tough and focused. She did not need all this sappy stuff. And unlike Grammy Rose's implication, she didn't have attics to clean out or walls to tear down, real or emotional.

Hoping to dispel the burgeoning well of unwanted feelings pressing against her chest, she shifted the tissue paper and unearthed a book on gardening and a set of crocheting needles. Suzanne laughed, relief spilling through her. Just as she'd thought—the items didn't suit her personality. She had a black thumb and couldn't even sew on a button, much less crochet.

Next she found a small black-velvet ring box. Her breath caught. She opened the delicate case and smiled at the note—''Sometimes, the simple things are the best.'' Her grandmother's very own gold wedding band winked at her beneath the Victorian lamplight. It was beautiful and so special that she would cherish it and keep it forever. But if she were getting married, she'd choose something much more showy. A big diamond solitaire or a huge sapphire with cut diamonds around the side. Or maybe an emerald.

Shaking her head at her own thoughts, she dug deeper into the hope chest, her eyes widening at her next discovery. A white lacy hat, shaped like a Stetson, with a white lace band and back bow, trimmed with silk roses, baby's breath and a feather. Next, came a pair of white Western lace-up boots, with hook-and-eye closures, two-and-a-half inch heels, narrow toes and a lace inset. And last but not least, a lace ribbon choker, adorned with iridescent flowers and dangling beads.

Suzanne tossed her head back and laughed outright. Grammy must have made a mistake when she'd put these things inside. Perhaps, she'd meant them for her cousins Angie or Caitlin. Suzanne was a city kind of girl. High heels and plunging necklines were more her style.

In fact, she'd use the choker to strangle herself before she'd marry someone who wanted a cowgirl bride.

Chapter One

Six Weeks Later

"Will you marry me, Suzanne?"

Suzanne gasped as her boss, James Horton, placed a dark-blue velvet box on top of the white satin tablecloth. They were seated at a table overlooking the lush gardens of the Cove at Chattahoochee, one of the most exclusive restaurants in Atlanta, and had just finished their gourmet meal of prime rib and salmon. Although romantic couples were plentiful in every corner, Suzanne and James had met to celebrate the closing of another megamillion-dollar deal completed by Horton Developers, not for a romantic tryst. At least that had been the plan.

Moonlight filtered through the picture windows, mingling with shades of greenery and the pinks and whites of the azaleas just starting to bloom. Red roses adorned all the tables, and a violin player strummed a classical tune softly in the background. Outside, the sound of the Chattahoochee River drifted through the sultry breeze, the pounding of water against rocks mimicking Suzanne's rapidly beating heart.

"I...I don't know what to say, James." Suzanne glanced into James's pale-green eyes which were twinkling mischievously, searching for some hint that he might be joking. Had some connection bubbled up between them while she wasn't looking? Granted, the atmosphere was romantic, the food and wine exquisite, and during the past few weeks, James had been extra solicitous of her when they'd wined and dined their clients, but marriage? She had never guessed he had the big *M* on his mind.

Sex, yes, although they hadn't yet consummated their relationship. But a long-lasting, loving relationship with mortgages and shared bank accounts? No, she definitely had not been prepared for a proposal.

James gestured toward the ring box, the deep laugh lines around his mouth twitching as he gauged her reaction. He had known she would be surprised, had counted on it. "Go ahead, open it. I think you'll like my selection."

Drawing in a calming breath, Suzanne tiptoed shaky fingers across the white linen and snagged the box, the soft velvet caressing her fingers. Tiffany's?

The moment she opened the box, her eyes widened with shock. A stunning sapphire flanked by diamond baguettes winked at her in the dim light. It was the exact ring she would have chosen for herself.

"Well, what do you think?"

Suzanne hadn't expected sentiment, but his pragmatic voice surprised her. "It's the most beautiful ring I've ever seen."

"You had me nervous for a minute." He pointed to the sapphire with a manicured finger. "There was a lovely emerald, but I thought this one suited you. It's your birthstone, right?"

"Yes. It's...perfect." She finally dragged her eyes from the shimmering stone to his face again. Softly chiseled features created a boy-next-door look, but a cutthroat businessman, not a tender heart, lay beneath. James was handsome, his suits tailored, his shoes imported Italian leather, his drive for success impressive. He was worldly, sophisticated, well-bred, well-mannered and well-off.

Everything a woman could want.

And there were lots of women in Atlanta who wanted him.

So, why was she even hesitating?

He took the ring and slipped it on the ring finger of her hand. "We have so much in common. We enjoy our work and we make a fabulous team, you have to admit that, and we like the same kinds of music and art and opera, and..." He hesitated, shrugging. "All in all, I think together we can take Horton Developers to the very top."

Suzanne frowned. All the things he'd said were true, but... Had she expected skyrockets to explode when a man proposed? A proclamation of undying passionate love to glide from his lips? She and James had never had that kind of relationship. Her father's words echoed in her ears—*Some of us don't ever find that hot romance, but that doesn't have to keep you from having a good partnership. Find someone who'll help you achieve your goals.*

"You don't have to answer me right now," he said. "In fact, as in any deal, you should take a few days to think it over."

She stared at the ring, then back at him, then back at the stunning sapphire. Did he really want to marry her or was he worried about losing her as a business partner?

He snapped the box lid closed and shifted deftly back to business. "Now, let's talk about how we can persuade Rafe McAllister to sell his ranch."

"MOTHER, THERE'S NO WAY I'm going to sell the Lazy M." Rafe McAllister winced at the worried expression on his sixty-year-old mother's wrinkled face. Her hand felt so frail in his, her pallor like buttermilk, her voice as weak as a child's.

"I know you don't want it to happen, son, but I also know we're in trouble here."

Rafe bit the inside of his cheek to keep from showing his reaction. "It's true, but we've had rough times before, Mom. We made it then and we'll make it now."

"That was before your daddy passed on, God rest his soul...."

Amen to that.

"Now..." She let the word trail off, fidgeting with the handmade quilt tucked over her shoulders. Another bout with her rheumatoid arthritis had sent her to bed three days ago.

Her implication stung him. Now what? She thought he was incompetent? That he could never live up to Frank McAllister's name?

If only his mother knew the truth....

But he didn't want to hurt her. And she would be hurt if she knew about her husband's betrayal. Frank McAllister had gambled away most of their life savings in a damn poker game. The rest had been used for the numerous women he chose to entertain when he was away. And then there was Rafe's mother's medical bills, which their insurance had not covered due to the fact that Frank hadn't made the last few monthly payments. Frank's indiscretions had forced Rafe to hang on to the family legacy as if it had been sewn with brittle thread.

The Lazy M meant everything to Rafe, and he'd go down fighting for it or die trying.

"I have to meet with Slim Wallace in Sugar Hill today to discuss refinancing the loan," Rafe said, interjecting a confidence into his voice he didn't feel. "Get some rest, Mom, I'll be back later."

She nodded, her gnarled hands tracing over the log-cabin pattern of the quilt. He kissed her cheek, then strode from the room, the problems mounting in his mind. He needed a new tractor, the fences had to be mended and he had to buy more cattle to expand the operation. Better feed would help his stock, too.

But everything took money.

The one thing he was plenty short of.

He jumped into the ugly purple pickup truck he'd won from Wiley Hartwell at his New Year's Eve bash, dusted off his jeans with one hand while he started the engine and slid it into gear. Maybe he'd find some help in Sugar Hill. Maybe he could sell this embarrassing grape-colored monstrosity for enough to spot a second mortgage. After all, small towns were supposed to embrace its own and help one another.

Hopefully the old-time values still held true, and he could avoid that heartless shark of a land developer who wanted to steal his property and turn his ranch into a damn shopping mall.

SUZANNE'S CONVERSATION with James played over and over in her head as she drove to Sugar Hill. *Do whatever it takes to get that land,* James had told Suzanne. *And when you do, there'll be a big bonus waiting for you. And a promotion.*

Suzanne had salivated at his promises. She had been working as an assistant for so long that she'd almost given up hope of moving up the chain of command. But today James had not only talked of a wifely partnership, but he'd mentioned a vice president position. As VP, her financial future would be secure, and she would have the respect of everyone at the company.

Especially since she had steered James toward the development opportunities near Sugar Hill.

Perhaps the mention of the promotion was one reason she had hesitated at James's proposal. She did not want to marry into the position; she wanted to earn it. To say she deserved it, not that she'd landed the position by sleeping with the boss.

The busy crowded streets of Atlanta faded behind her as she left the expressway and steered her sports car toward Sugar Hill. The suburbs flanking the city and mini shopping centers finally gave way to farmland and more sparsely populated areas, turning green with the approaching spring. The quiet melody of cows mooing and crickets chirping replaced city traffic noises, the sun setting in a rainbow of colors.

James had laid out his plans for the gigantic multistore shopping mall with its neighboring strip shopping centers and businesses, and of course, homes and apartments which would undoubtedly crop up once people discovered jobs in the area. The development would boost the economy of Sugar Hill, as well, the reason Suzanne had suggested looking at the area. James had narrowed the choices for the project down to three parcels of land, but Rafe McAllister's ranch was the largest and offered easiest access to the main highway. Basically the Lazy M was the property James really wanted.

And James always got what he wanted.

She wouldn't let him down this time, either.

Although she had joked with Rebecca about approaching Rafe McAllister, Rebecca had warned her that she'd heard he'd been a troublemaker in school. He was also stubborn and had staunchly refused James's previous generous offers.

The rancher had fallen on hard times, though, and was in big trouble financially. As always, James had done his homework. He had full financial reports on the man as well as personal information that would tip the scales and convince Rafe to sell. Something about Rafe's father's shady past.

Suzanne sincerely hoped none of that information had to be used to persuade McAllister. She understood big business but she hated the dirty side of it. Still, selling the Lazy M to Horton Developers would not only benefit Rafe, but the development would help Sugar Hill's economy. Once people discovered the charm the small town offered, coupled with its proximity to a major shopping mecca, they would flock to live there. Uncle Wiley's business, Alison's bridal shop and Mimi's and Rebecca's bookstore/café would all benefit.

Excitement bloomed in her chest at the possibilities. No matter how stubborn Rafe McAllister was, she had to win him over to her way of thinking.

RAFE'S MOTHER ALWAYS SAID that when it rained it poured. Well, it was hailing cats and dogs as far as Rafe was concerned. Before he'd left for the bank, two of his best steers had escaped. Finally he'd received a call from the sheriff's department that his most prized animal was standing in the middle of a six-lane highway creating a ten-mile traffic jam. Before long he and his hired hand had lured the stubborn animal back to the pasture. It had taken two hours and two hundred dollars of fencing material to repair the damage. Not to mention what it had cost his leg. His old injury throbbed like the devil.

Then, when he'd finally arrived at the bank three hours late for the meeting, an already-ticked-off Slim Wallace had turned down his loan and given him thirty days to catch up on his payments—or else. Rafe had gone straight to the newspaper and placed an ad to sell the purple truck, but Georgiana Hamilton had laughed, knowing that selling the sissified vehicle was a long shot. Then he'd run into Old Man Perkinson who owned the drugstore and learned his credit had expired. No more of his mother's medication without cash.

What else could go wrong today?

Deciding to nurse his troubles with a beer, he strode into the Dusty Pub. Country music blared from the jukebox, peanut shells discarded on the floor crunched beneath his boots, and the clatter of beer mugs and laughter rang above the hum of voices. All in all, it was a usual Saturday night. Old cowpokes hovered over the scarred wooden bar, three or four younger ranch hands shot pool in the back corner, cracking jokes and eyeing the women, and cigarette smoke mingled with the scent of perfume from the handful of females who graced the joint.

Johnny Wakefield, the thirty-something bartender, slid a cold mug overflowing with beer onto the counter. Rafe nodded his thanks, his gaze catching sight of a tall female in tight, crisp new jeans and platform shoes sauntering from the ladies' room to-

ward the bar. She slid onto a stool at a small round
table in the corner, her sexy butt hugging the vinyl
just the way a man would want to hug her. Her too-
tight lacy shirt spelled sex appeal, her designer jeans
and shoes spelled money, and the slight tilt to her
dainty nose spelled sophistication.

What the hell was she doing in the Dusty Pub?

"Her name's Suzanne Hartwell," Johnny offered
before he could even ask. "Her daddy's some high-
falutin doctor in Atlanta."

And she probably lived off Daddy's money. That
explained the attitude. He'd seen it before.

"Every man in the place has been drooling over
her since she strutted in."

"I'll bet." Like she would give any of them the
time of day. "What's she doing here anyway? Come
slumming in the country?"

"Her sister Rebecca lives in Sugar Hill. Wiley
Hartwell's her uncle."

Somehow this woman didn't look related to that
outlandish uncle of hers, though. And he'd met her
sister, Rebecca, in that bookstore. She was pretty but
quiet, sort of shy.

Not like a siren waiting to be noticed. And Rafe
had noticed. Any red-blooded male would.

Especially a bad-boy bachelor at heart. In fact, he
liked slow country music, fast women and wild
horses—not necessarily in that order.

She pivoted on the stool, and his gut clenched as
if one of his horses had kicked him. Following on

cue, his leg throbbed, a reminder of just how dangerous their kick could be, too.

A heart-shaped slender face with dark exotic eyes stared back at him, her small, pink lips curling into a sexy smile. Raven hair hung past her shoulders like a thick, silky mane, adding to the sultry enchantment of her almond-shaped eyes. She was trouble with a capital *T*, the kind of woman he'd normally avoid.

The kind who had burned him in the past.

"What's the lady drinking?" his traitorous mouth asked.

"White wine." Johnny chuckled. "'Course, first she asked for one of them fancy drinks, a Cosmopolitan or something. When I told her we didn't have that, she wanted something called Sex on the Beach. Imagine her asking for something like that in Sugar Hill."

Rafe's mouth quirked up. Yeah, she might get more than she'd bargained for. Not that he knew exactly what Sex on the Beach was.

"Finally settled for wine."

"Send her a glass from me."

Johnny laughed again. "I figured you'd be the only one bold enough to actually try and pick her up."

Rafe nodded, in spite of the fact that his brain was screaming at him to leave her alone. Bold or stupid? It was a fine line. The men in the bar would probably be laughing in a second when she snubbed her nose at him.

But to his surprise, Suzanne Hartwell accepted the

drink, then shocked him even more by crooking one of her long slender fingers for him to join her. He tipped his Stetson in reply, then ordered a second beer and strode toward her, his heart pounding like a runaway stallion.

His day had just gotten a whole lot better. Maybe he could forget his money troubles for the night. After all, even if Suzanne Hartwell was out of his league, a simple flirtation might ease the sting from his godawful day.

Chapter Two

Suzanne's fingers tightened around the stem of the wineglass as Rafe McAllister slowly strode toward her. She would do as James suggested—keep her part in the company a secret until she got to know Rafe. Thanks to James's extensive report, she had known just where to find him. The Dusty Pub, a little honky-tonk on the edge of town.

She had never seen such a powerful man or one with such wicked intent in the bold set of his walk. Jet-black hair, shaggy and unkempt, curled around the bottom of his neck, and his high cheekbones accentuated his solemn expression. She tried to get a peek at his eyes, but they lay hidden beneath the brim of his black Stetson. Instinctively she knew they would be as dark and brooding as the aura of masculinity surrounding him. Rafe McAllister was a real-life cowboy.

A denim workshirt hugged his broad shoulders, the top two buttons undone so dark curls of hair whorled in the opening. His hands were large and callused, a testament to the fact that he worked outside, and even white teeth gleamed against his tanned face as he offered her a lopsided smile. A smile meant to seduce and disarm a woman from all her defenses.

She sipped her wine, working to swallow, as her gaze drifted south. Dusty, worn jeans strained against muscular thighs, and cowboy boots that looked ancient showcased his devil-may-care stride. There was no denying that he was a well-made man.

He cleared his throat, his voice a low, sexy rumble as he tipped his hat in a gentlemanly gesture, "Howdy, ma'am. Rafe McAllister."

Suzanne fought a nervous chuckle at his drawl, but looked up into his eyes and stifled her laughter. Just as she'd imagined, they were dark and serious, but amber flecks streaked the irises, the golden brown the color of the whiskey her father drank at bedtime. With a shiver, she remembered that scotch went down as smooth as silk, but then sparked a burning all the way through your toes.

She uncurled hers where they had turned under from his hot gaze. "Hi, I'm Suzanne Hartwell."

"I heard." He gestured toward the bartender. "Every man in here knows your name, sugar."

She did smile this time. "It's always nice to be noticed."

He laughed, a thick throaty sound that made her heart flutter. Mercy me, Suzanne thought, mimicking Grammy Rose's favorite expression. Rafe McAllister was nothing like the rancher she'd expected. She could easily see how he'd earned his troublemaker image years ago. In high school, every mother within a hundred-mile radius had probably warned their daughters away from the man.

The country music continued to wail, a song about looking for love in all the wrong places that described her disastrous dating life in a nutshell, while Rafe slid onto the barstool, spreading his legs outward causing one of his knees to rest against her thigh.

Suzanne resisted the urge to move. Rafe McAllister was not supposed to affect her this way. After all, she needed the upper hand with him, not the other way around.

Plus she was *almost* engaged, wasn't she?

He propped his elbow on the battered wooden tabletop. "So, what brings you to Sugar Hill?"

You. Suzanne bit back the truth. "I stopped in to visit some of my relatives. My sister, Rebecca, runs the bookstore, she just got married a few weeks ago. How about you? Do you live around here, cowboy?"

He nodded. "I own the Lazy M Ranch right outside of town. I've met your uncle Wiley."

She grinned. "Everyone knows him." She ran a finger along the rim of her glass. "Hey, didn't you win that purple pickup truck on New Year's Eve?"

"That would be me." For the first time since he'd sat down, his smile faded slightly.

"You don't like the truck?"

He lifted his broad shoulders into a shrug. "It runs great, and it's loaded on the inside. But the color..."

"Not what a rancher would have chosen."

"Exactly."

"You could have it painted."

"Probably will."

He finished his beer and she waved to the bartender to bring him another. "My treat this time."

"No." He placed a hand over hers before she could reach for her wallet.

"It's just a beer," Suzanne said, surprised at the stubborn thrust of his chin. "It is the twenty-first century. Women buy men drinks all the time."

"Maybe in the city," Rafe said in a gruff voice. "But not in Sugar Hill." Pride laced his voice. Now she understood him. He was the old-fashioned, Southern-bred type with barrels of macho pride that would make it difficult for him to admit defeat and sell out.

So, why did a seed of admiration stir inside her? Because she understood about pride. Still, most of the men she'd dated thought nothing of going dutch or letting her buy dinner and drinks. In fact, in some ways, sharing the bill had become the norm.

He shoved a twenty on the counter and indicated for Johnny to freshen her drink, as well. Suzanne tried to drag her eyes away and focus on the patrons. Locals were heading to the dance floor, two-stepping and line dancing to the popular melody, laughing and flirting. Rafe's knee jerked up and down in time with the music as if he enjoyed the country tunes. Suzanne had always thought country music too twangy. Songs about cheating wives and sick dogs howling in the back of pickups with sawed-off shotguns lodged over the cab were just not her cup of tea. Give her Elton John or Dave Matthews any day.

Forget the music. Make chitchat, Suzanne. You're here to get him to talk about himself. He has no idea you already know half of his life story. "So, Rafe, you have a big spread around here?"

He nodded, tilting the beer mug up for a sip, once again drawing her attention to the strong muscles in his jaw. "A few hundred acres. I raise some cattle. Got a few cutting horses, too."

"I've always wanted to learn to ride."

"Really?" A chuckle rumbled from his chest, mischief dancing in his eyes as he angled his head and swept a look over her. "Well, sugar, come on out to the Lazy M. I'll be glad to saddle a mare and teach you."

She met his challenge with a teasing look of her own. "Maybe I'll do that."

"Maybe you should."

"Do you want to dance?" Suzanne clenched her glass in midair, hardly able to believe she'd just blurted out that invitation. But dancing with the man might ease her tension and help her refocus. She'd come to Sugar Hill on a mission; she couldn't let this sexy bad boy sidetrack her. He probably collected women like a little boy collected toy cars, then threw them away the minute the paint faded.

Hunger flared in Rafe's eyes. Good. At least she wasn't the only one feeling flashes of desire. The realization sent need soaring through her like an aphrodisiac.

The music mellowed from a fast tune to a slow, sultry melody, and several more couples joined those on the dance floor, their bodies tucked tightly together. Still, he hesitated. His gaze caught her ring. "That depends. I don't encroach on another man's territory."

Suzanne bit her tongue. "No one owns me, Rafe."

A grin tugged at his mouth. "All right, then." He offered a massive hand and she slipped hers inside, then allowed him to lead her to the dance floor. His hard boots clicked on the wood planks as he pulled her into his arms and began to lull her into the rhythm of the song. She thought she'd detected a slight limp for a minute, but it disappeared so quickly she decided she'd imagined it.

Suzanne had gone clubbing with her girlfriends and James at the trendiest spots in the city, but she had never been as hypnotized by a song as she was in Rafe's arms. They circled the dance floor, his big body moving seductively against hers, denim-clad legs brushing denim, the warmth of his breath whispering against her neck as he held her close. Her heart pounded inside her chest, and at five-seven for the first time in her life she felt small next to a man.

This was not going as planned.

She was supposed to be talking to him, learning his weak spot, and moving in to find out how to trap him into selling his land. Not falling under some kind of hypnotic spell.

"You feel like heaven," he whispered roughly.

He felt like heaven, too. Suzanne closed her eyes

and forgot about the land deal and the fact that yesterday another man had proposed to her.

Because for just a moment she wanted to savor being in this man's arms and not think about work.

RAFE THREADED his fingers through the long strands of Suzanne's silky hair, his breath locking in his chest.

A fierce need to possess her overcame him, unlike anything he'd ever felt before.

She was soft and sensuous and had the voice of a vamp. And God help him, he could get lost in those exotic brown eyes. They were like a sea of hot chocolate, rich and dark and mesmerizing.

But holding her was all wrong.

She was a Hartwell, the niece of a well-known town member, the daughter of a prominent Atlanta doctor. A rich, well-bred girl with more money and more education than him. For goodness' sake, the damn sapphire ring on her hand alone could pay for all sorts of farm equipment, not to mention that her hands were delicate, uncallused, and she was used to men with hands that weren't hardened or dirt-stained from the land. And damn it, she didn't seem like the footloose and fancy-free type that slept around, either.

And right now he had nothing to offer any woman except a one-night stand.

Suzanne Hartwell would undoubtedly want more. He knew her type. Driven by career, not family. She

wanted the nice things in life. Things he had no way
to give a woman.

Plus, her daddy would probably kill him if he
found her dancing with a run-down cowboy in a dive
called the Dusty Pub.

As if to cement his reservations, the door to the
bar opened and in walked Slim Wallace, the man
who'd told Rafe in no uncertain terms today that he
was going to lose everything. Slim's words scraped
over his consciousness like a razor over raw skin—
*You might as well declare bankruptcy. Let me take
over the ranch and move on, Rafe. It's too late.*

Damn it. It wasn't too late. The Lazy M was *his*
ranch. *His* legacy. The land had belonged to his father and his daddy before him and his daddy before
him. Somehow they had all managed to hold on to
the place because the McAllisters believed that if a
man had land, he had a place to build a life. Without
it, a man couldn't survive.

And he would not be the one to let it all go.

He suddenly realized the music had stopped. Suzanne had stilled in his arms and was looking up at
him with big doe eyes, her expensive perfume so
intoxicating he'd pulled her to him in a viselike grip.
He glanced down in horror, immediately releasing
her. He could not drown his sorrows in her soft,
tempting body.

"I'm sorry."

"What's wrong?" she asked in a low voice.

He shook his head. His problems were his own. A

woman like Suzanne Hartwell would never understand.

They had shared one dance. That was all they
would ever have.

SUZANNE STOOD on the dance floor alone in stunned
disbelief as Rafe slipped out the barroom door. After
that soul-hugging dance, he had mumbled a hasty
apology and a goodbye, claiming he had forgotten
something he needed to do, then run for the door as
if she had suddenly pulled out handcuffs and tried to
arrest him.

Had something really come up? Something to do
with his ranch? His sick mother?

She tried not to think about the ailing Mrs. McAllister.

The thought resurrected memories of her own
mother, those last few days of her illness stirring the
hot pot of emotions that always simmered close to
the surface at the thought of her.

Refusing to allow the pot to boil over, she wove
through the crowd and found her table, then slumped
down on the bar stool, wishing she'd had more time
with Rafe.

To pump him for information, she told herself. Not
to dance or hold him or dream about finding heaven
in his arms.

Steepling her hands tent-style and leaning her head
into them, she closed her eyes and shut out the images that swirled through her mind, steeling herself
back in control. She hated feeling vulnerable. James

had taught her to attack, to go in for the kill, to eliminate the human element of a business situation, evaluate all the data, make a decision and move on it. Her father used the same approach.

The technique had always worked for her before.

She wanted to earn her promotion. She would use the tried-and-true methods to do so now, and forget emotion, and the way Rafe's lips might taste.

Just as soon as the memory of his hands on her waist and his breath on her neck subsided.

"You want another drink?" Johnny asked.

Suzanne shook her head. "No, I think I'll call it a night."

"Stick around and we can hang out after I shut down."

Suzanne's gaze shot to his.

"I promise not to run out on you like Rafe. Poor guy's got a lot on his mind today."

Okay, he had offered the bait and she was fishing. "Why, did something happen?"

"Heard Wallace turned down his loan. It's just a matter of time before he loses the Lazy M."

And Horton Developers would be there to save him, Suzanne thought. It would be the best thing for both of them.

"Has he spoken to anyone about selling the property?" Suzanne asked.

Johnny shrugged. "Some big developer from Atlanta, but he turned him down flat. Can't stand the thought of a big mall going in where his cattle have grazed all his life. Supposed to be a town meeting to discuss the proposed development in the morning.''

''Really?''

''Yeah, some of the town's all for it, but others think it'll bring sin and crime to Sugar Hill.''

Oh, heavens, didn't they see the good the development would bring to their little town? That change was not always negative, but progress meant positive things for the people and community?

''Where is this town meeting going to be held?''

''City hall. Noon.''

Suzanne smiled and patted his hand, then stood and said goodbye. ''Thanks, Johnny. The drinks were great.''

She'd stay over in Sugar Hill tonight and be at that town meeting tomorrow. She wanted to hear what everyone had to say.

Especially the sexy cowboy with the whiskey-colored bedroom eyes.

Chapter Three

As usual, Rafe rose early the next morning, knowing he had to finish his chores and clean up before lunch to make it to the town meeting by noon. He and his two hands, Bud and Red, had finished moving the cattle to the east grazing pasture, then Bud and Red stopped to repair the fencing that had been torn down by the last ice storm along the northern border of his property. Rafe rode Thunder, his prized stallion, across the rolling hills toward the ranch house, the fresh scent of hay and dirt soothing to his weary state.

He had not slept well the night before.

Dreams of dancing with Suzanne Hartwell had haunted his sleep. He could still smell the sultry essence of her expensive perfume and feel the satiny softness of her hair tickling his chin. And those subtle curves. Oh, at first she'd looked like a bony model, but beneath those stiff designer clothes, he'd sensed a softness that had melted into the hard planes of his own body. A softness and passion that had turned him inside out. Unbridled hunger, sass, spunk—Suzanne Hartwell was no shy, wimpy female. Pampered and spoiled, yes. But defenseless and naive—no way. Making love to her would be like taming a wild horse, he imagined. Or dancing with the wolves.

The reason she was off-limits.

Rich, city women could never understand the kind of life he led, the love of the land, the adrenaline that kept him alive as he worked with his hands. The pleasure that pumped through him as he listened to the night sounds of the farm, the cows, the crickets, the blissful quiet of a hot summer's night. The primitive raw power he thrived on by living off the land, by mastering a wild stallion.

Yep, Suzanne Hartwell was the wrong kind of woman to play footsie with. She was not a nature-loving, horse kind of girl, but a mall-loving, diamond-studded piece of eye candy. He should never have indulged his wanderlust by flirting with her, should never have held her in his arms.

Hell, he didn't have time to indulge himself with any woman right now, especially one like her. His ranch needed major work. And now with his mother's health failing, the inside of the house was deteriorating, too. Maria, the Hispanic woman he'd recently hired to help out, was nice enough, but she'd dyed all his undershorts pink. Apparently she didn't have a good grasp of laundry skills.

Pink undershorts were the least of his worries.

Hopefully, some of the townsfolk would rally to

his side against the idea of the new development. At least stalling the project would help get that developer off his back for a while. Maybe then Slim Wallace would cut him some slack. Knowing Rafe had a buyer made it way too easy for Slim to play hardball and lower the ax on Rafe. *Sell,* Slim had told him. *Sell it and get out of debt.*

Then where would Rafe be?

He would have nothing. His hands tightened on the horse's reins as he let Thunder guide him over the ridge. His land stretched for miles, the lush green North Georgia mountains rising in front of him, the thick pines and hardwoods and apple houses in the distance a reminder of his heritage. He had grown up here, ridden this same stretch with his grandfather and listened to his stories of the old pioneer days of his forefathers. He wanted to pass that heritage along to his son one day.

Today he would fight for himself and the preservation of Sugar Hill. Let Suzanne Hartwell have the city. Hopefully, she'd already gone back to Atlanta, with its fancy shops and smog and traffic, where she belonged.

"YES, JAMES, I'm almost there." Cell phone in hand, Suzanne squinted through the high noon sun as she drove toward city hall. "I'm right on time for that town meeting."

"Good. I want a full report so we know what we're up against, especially if those small-towners

protest the development," James said. "Have you
met Rafe McAllister yet?"

"Yes."

"Do you think he's bending any?"

"It's too early to tell."

"Well, I know you, honey. You can charm the
pants off any man."

If he didn't charm her pants off first. Annoyance
hit her as James' comment sank in. "James, you
aren't suggesting…?"

"No, of course not, that was just a figure of
speech."

"Good. Because I have no intention of seducing
some man just to steal his property from him." Of
course, seducing him for pleasure had crossed her
mind the night before.

Quickly, Suzanne tried to change the subject.
"How about Forrest Anderson? Did he agree to
sell?"

"Yes, but his neighbor Will Samuels refused. And
we need both properties to have enough land to complete the proposed site." James sighed. "Even if they
agreed, neither piece of land is as nice as McAllister's or as convenient to the interstate. I can already
envision the houses we could build on that side of
the mountain."

"The property is pretty spectacular," Suzanne admitted, although she still couldn't imagine moving
out to the country. She liked the bustle of midtown,
the art shows and theaters and nightclubs. Although,
the traffic definitely got on her nerves. Where would

James want to live if she accepted his proposal and they married? His home in Buckhead was nice but cold, and far from homey.

The sapphire ring sparkled from her right hand where she'd decided to wear it until she made a decision. So far James hadn't pressured her for an answer to his proposal. And she didn't expect him to, not until this deal was settled.

Business always came first with James.

Not that she could blame him. He had a fortune riding on this project. She hung up with him and studied the fading chipped paint of some of the downtown area. Alison's bridal shop, Weddings to Remember, had been freshly painted, and the Hotspot, Mimi and Rebecca's bookstore/café had new awnings, but some of the other buildings desperately needed facelifts. The new development would definitely boost the economy and enable the locals to update their own businesses. She mentally added the argument to her list as she parked in front of city hall. Already cars, SUVs and minivans overflowed the parking lot. Slim Wallace, the head of the bank, raced in, yanking at his baggy trousers.

As soon as she entered the meeting room, she felt the tension in the air. Her uncle Wiley stood at the front of the room, clad in his signature lime-green jacket and checkered pants. Cousins Hannah, Mimi, Alison and their husbands occupied front row seats. Her sister Rebecca and Thomas sat behind them, and locals filled the other rows of chairs. A few she rec-

ognized from her short visits into Sugar Hill, but
most were strangers.

The hair on the back of her neck suddenly prick-
led, and she glanced to her left. Standing against the
far back wall, looking tall and imposing in his dusty
jeans, with his black Stetson tipped low on his head,
stood Rafe McAllister. And from the dark stare he
slanted her way, he didn't look pleased to see her.

WHAT THE HELL was Suzanne Hartwell doing at a
Sugar Hill town meeting?

Rafe glared at her, irritated that she'd gotten under
his skin. She had no reason to be here, no right to
get involved in the town's business.

No right to stir his libido and make him want
things he couldn't have.

The mayor, Orville Lewis, a portly man with a
bald spot as big as Rafe's fist, called the meeting to
order. "We're here to discuss the future of Sugar
Hill," Mayor Lewis said.

"You mean the demise," Carter Anderson, the
owner of the local dry cleaners, yelled.

His comment started everyone talking and shouting and arguing at once.

"We have to put a stop to this land developer
coming in and taking over our town!" an elderly
man shouted.

"I moved here to get away from the city. There's
too much noise and traffic in Atlanta," a middle-
aged man in a gray suit said. "And now folks want
to build a big mall that will draw crowds out here."

"Cars'll be clogging our roads, blowing exhaust into the air and bringing all kinds of derelicts around," a frail woman in a pink knit dress exclaimed.

"But it would be nice not to have to drive two or three hours to buy school clothes for the kids," Mrs. Ludwig, mother of five, argued.

Myrtle Lowercrust, the children's church choir director stood up. "The kids won't have the country air to breathe and the space to run and play."

"Be a bunch of cookie-cutter houses and apartments everywhere," her sister, Ethel, added.

"But we'll have movie theaters and restaurants to choose from, and maybe even a nice dance studio that will offer some culture to this backward town," another woman protested.

"Our town is not backward." Hannah Hartwell Tippins placed a hand over her rounded belly. "We have good hometown values. And safe streets for the children."

"Some progress is good," Rebecca's husband, Dr. Thomas Emerson, pointed out. "Maybe we could compromise and find a happy medium. I'm sure you people want the best medical care available."

"We have a good hospital," Alison pointed out. "And Brady runs the medical helicopter service for emergencies."

"I want my kids to smell fresh air and see the wildflowers on the mountains in the spring," Rebecca said. "Not have high-rises and concrete blocking the views."

Wiley Hartwell flapped his arms like a peacock. "We don't need strangers coming in, starting up businesses that will take away from our own. My car dealership, the local hardware store, they'll all be run off by corporations and chains."

"You men are just worried about your wallets," Wanita Rivers, Rafe's mother's friend, said. "Maybe we women would like to dress in style for a change, not have to shop at the outlet mall for last year's throwaways."

"Think about the jobs a new mall would bring," Vivian Hartwell said.

"Yeah, then all our kids wouldn't have to leave Sugar Hill to find jobs," a young mother shouted.

"My filling station would probably pick up business," Eke Turner added.

"But with it comes more crime," Jake Tippins, Hannah's husband and now town sheriff, pointed out.

The mayor beat his gavel, yelling for order, but the women from the Prayer Wagon burst through the door, then stomped across the crowded room, bouncing homemade protest signs and banners in the air. "Stop the development! Leave Sugar Hill be."

Jean Ann Tucker, spokeswoman for the group, raised a bull horn. "We don't want this mall. It'll bring sleazy nightclubs and strip joints and those awful bars where people get shot!"

Anita Haynes flopped a hand dramatically over her bosom. "There'll be raping and pillaging in the streets!"

Rafe grinned to himself, grateful for all the drama

queens. He opened his mouth to voice his opinion when Suzanne Hartwell suddenly shot to the front of the room. What the hell was she doing?

HEAVENS ALIVE! Suzanne had heard enough. These people were about to create a panic like nothing she'd ever seen. ''You're imagining the worst, when you should consider all the benefits this development will offer.'' Suzanne kept her voice calm, well aware half of the town was shooting daggers at her while the other half nodded her on.

''Many positive things result from a new development. While petty crimes might increase slightly and a few nightclubs might spring up close to the mall, they'll be so far out of town they won't detract from the culture of Sugar Hill. The retail jobs the various establishments would offer and tourists they would attract would be invaluable. Just think of the tax revenues and employment opportunities. Construction, security positions, opportunities for web designers, buyers, decorating firms, the list is endless. And don't forget that the town's economy has been sliding the last few years. All the downtown stores need updating. More people moving to town would be a major boost to the economy. Consider the advantages you can give your children with added revenues. You can finally put computers in the schools and modernize the classrooms.''

Rafe McAllister stalked toward her, propped his hands on his hips and glared down at her. She was certainly passionate about her arguments, but she was on the wrong damn side of the issue. "You don't even live in this town, Ms. Hartwell, so why do you think you have the right to tell people what to do?"

A few patrons in back amened his comment. Suzanne twisted sideways, jerking her head to stare into his eyes. He towered over her, but she refused to let him intimidate her. "Half of my family lives here, Mr. McAllister. Besides, I'm simply pointing out things to help everyone make an informed, rational decision."

"Your opinion doesn't matter," Rafe said, jamming his face angrily in hers. "So why don't you flit back to the city you love so much, and let the people who live in this town decide what they want?"

"Here, here," a few angry locals shouted.

"Let's have some order," the mayor yelled, slamming his gavel down again. "I say we table this discussion for now. Everyone has brought up some interesting points. I'll appoint a committee to explore all sides, and we'll reconvene in a week to discuss it further."

The crowd applauded, then began to disperse. Rafe pulled Suzanne outside. "Why are you nosing in here when this is none of your business? You don't live or work here."

Suzanne tensed, glancing down at her arm where his fingers held her. Had he figured out she was working for Horton Developers?

Part of her wanted to admit the truth about her intentions, to lay her cards on the table, but the other part wasn't prepared for his wrath. She needed to focus before she revealed her part in the development. She needed to get to know him better and find that weak spot.

If he had one.

Landing this promotion would give her the independence and the financial security she wanted. And she'd make her father proud, something she'd strived for all her life. She couldn't let Rafe interfere because he was too stubborn to realize that change was good.

"I suppose you're so simpleminded that you'd return to the way the town was a hundred years ago. Forget the cars and electric appliances, let's all drive wagons and wash our clothes by beating them on the rocks!"

"Simpleminded? You think ranching is simpleminded work?"

He stepped forward, planting the hard wall of his chest against her. Fury blazed in his eyes as he pinned her still. "Just who do you think you are? Do you even have a job or do you let Daddy pay your bills?"

Suzanne's breath wheezed out, but she didn't back down. "My father does not support me, Mr. McAllister. I work…in an office and raise money for charities." Not exactly a lie. She did help her father host several charity parties.

"You have no idea how beautiful the mountains are around here, do you?" His gruff voice skated over her nerve endings, his words evoking images of him and mountain peaks, riding off into a sunset, bareback and bare chested.

Good Lord, what in the world was wrong with her?

"The mayor has given everyone a week to think about this. Did you know it's my property that developer wants to destroy?"

"Really?" Suzanne played dumb.

"Really." Rafe's fingers were still wound tight around her arm. " I dare you to come out and see my spread, ride across the land, smell the air and the mountains and then advocate turning my ranch into a damn shopping mall."

"All right, I will." Suzanne aimed her seductive smile at him. The dare would be a piece of cake. While she was riding the land, she'd be able to point out all the advantages to selling. And before the week ended she'd have him eating out of the palm of her hand.

There was no way she'd lose a dare to this infuriating man. Or anything else.

No matter how sexy he was....

Chapter Four

Rafe stared at the puffy white clouds billowing in the velvety blue sky of North Georgia, breathing in the smell of the grass as his hand tightened around the wooden sign he'd just finished carving. After he and his ranch hands had finished their morning rounds, Bud had suggested boarding horses and offering riding lessons as a way to increase the cash flow. Although Rafe agreed it was a decent idea, the thought of teaching irked him. As a teen, he had spent endless grueling hours working on a dude ranch, aiding the snobby, rich girls who'd wanted to learn to ride but who had balked at the smell of a horse and the feel of his hands on them after hours. And asking them to muck out a stall had been the kiss of death.

That was what the hired hands were supposed to do. *His* hands.

Except for one blonde, Cecilia. She had a way of making a man *want* to do the dirty work for her. Cecilia hadn't minded his hands on her at all. In fact, she'd liked playing with fire, and had danced the flame right underneath her father's patrician nose, teasing her father and him with her bold defiance. But her walk on the wild side had burned Rafe. Bad.

He'd been weary of that type of woman ever since.

The noonday sun beat down on him as he grabbed a hammer and strode down his long driveway to the mailbox beside the road. He drove the post into the ground and angled it so anyone driving by could read it. The newspaper ad started today, as well.

Filling his lungs with fresh, clean air, he gazed out over the two hundred acres of green pastures. The scents of hay and horses and grass filled his nostrils like an aphrodisiac. The only thing that smelled sweeter was a woman.

Suzanne Hartwell.

He hadn't slept for thinking about her all night. And that damn expensive perfume.

A perfume that would make a rational man senseless. He slammed the hammer against the post to dig it in more securely. Why the hell had she stuck her nose in where it didn't belong?

Would she take him up on his dare?

He hoped not. He hoped she climbed in whatever kind of fancy car she drove and hightailed it back to Atlanta, leaving him to deal with his troubles. He did not need a distraction like her around.

Yet, she *was* a Hartwell, and if he swayed her to his side, maybe she could convince the rest of the Hartwell clan to protest that developer's ideas and keep that blasted mall away from Sugar Hill.

Not a bad plan.

He pounded the hammer again, but heard a motor and looked up, curious as to who owned the automobile zooming toward his place. With his ranch situated on the outskirts of town, he rarely had visitors. The composure he'd been trying so hard to assimilate disintegrated when he spotted sassy Suzanne Hartwell veering toward him in a sporty little silver Miata, her ebony hair blowing in the wind.

SUZANNE SCANNED the picturesque view of the mountain ranges that served as a backdrop for Rafe McAllister's ranch, her mind already envisioning the hub of cars and visitors to the mall that would replace the old farmhouse and the shabby-looking barn. Adrenaline surged through her in a giddy roar as she imagined the designer shoe shops and dress boutiques. The barn would make a perfect location for the rustic outdoor company which would sell recreational equipment and clothing, camping, fishing, hunting and backpacking supplies as well as the climbing wall and skateboarding center already in the design phases.

And Suzanne's favorite—an old-fashioned carousel with hand-painted horses and buggies, which would sit center stage to the eatery like a giant music box. In her mind's eye she could see the beautiful swirls of color as the horses spun around, the excited shrieks of the children as they climbed onboard for a ride. And of course, the huge eatery would offer a wide variety of meals and refreshments to entice customers to spend more time and money, which equaled more revenue for the town. Everyone would benefit.

On closer scrutiny, the house's wraparound porch—with its swing and rockers—looked idyllic, like a Norman Rockwell postcard, but the house obviously needed repairs. Perhaps the construction company could renovate the house, turn it into a restaurant that served country meals, adding small-town ambience to the tourist's day of shopping. She made a mental note to add the idea to her list of suggestions to give James as she stopped in front of Rafe McAllister's mailbox and the homemade sign advertising for boarders and offering riding lessons.

He must be seriously distressed over his finances or he wouldn't have resorted to such lengths to make a dollar. She had to convince him that Horton Developers had come to rescue him not destroy his life. She pumped the brake, and the Miata rolled to a stop beside him. Tucking her windblown hair behind one ear, she smiled and said, "Hi."

He tipped his battered black Stetson, those dark enigmatic eyes skating over her with less than approval.

Suzanne wet her lips. "I came to take you up on your invitation."

"Excuse me?"

She jutted her chin up in the air. "To see your place. I believe it was a dare."

A small smile tugged at his firmly set lips. Rafe McAllister might be attracted to her physically, but she sensed that for some reason, he didn't *like* her or particularly welcome the attraction.

The realization stung, but she shrugged it away. She hadn't come here to get him to like her, anyway; she would simply schmooze enough to parlay the heated discussion they'd begun at the town meeting into a congenial business deal that would leave everyone happy and satisfied.

And elevate her a rung on the corporate ladder.

"Then drive on up to the house and we'll get started."

Suzanne gestured toward the passenger seat of her car, stuffing the tags to her new designer Stetson lying on the leather seat into the console. "Climb in, cowboy, and I'll give you a ride."

He shot a skeptical look toward the gray leather. "Take longer for me to fold my legs in and out of that matchbox than it will for me to walk."

And just like that, he expressed his disapproval of her car as well. Suzanne barely resisted the urge to gun the engine and spit gravel and dust in his face as she cruised behind him. He walked up the drive with long easy strides, ignoring her. However, she noticed the occasional tightening of his mouth and realized the slight limp she'd detected at the bar that night was real. It obviously still caused him pain.

Instead of retaliating against his rudeness, though, she opted for saccharine sweetness and pure male flattery. "You do have long legs. How tall are you, Rafe?"

He smirked as if he knew what she was doing and didn't intend to fall for it. "Six-three."

"With the boots."

"Without."

Big hands. Big feet. Big everything. Including a big bad attitude.

She was going to have her hands full with this one.

Seconds later she parked beside the house and climbed out, chasing after him as he headed toward the barn. The pointed toes of her spit-shiny, red-and-black handcrafted boots pinched her feet as she dodged the pockets of horse dung scattered along the fence and tried to keep up with him.

HOW THE HELL could one saucy little woman make him feel like horse manure? Especially one wearing too tight, brand-spanking-new designer jeans, and a fifty-dollar red-and-black-plaid shirt that matched those silly looking dress-for-show snakeskin high-heeled boots? She probably had a Porter Wagner fringed jacket in the trunk of that pea-size thing she called a car.

And while she smelled like sweetness and jasmine, he smelled like dirt and cattle.

Damn it, he'd seen the look of condemnation on Suzanne's face as if she thought his home was an eyesore that should be bulldozed down and landscaped with cookie-cutter condos and manicured lawns. Lawns barely big enough to hold a lounge chair much less house a neighborhood barbecue. He'd read about cul de sac parties in the suburbs where the homeowners congregated with cheap grills so they could watch their kids play in the streets because they didn't have anyplace else to do so. He would not allow his property to be turned into one of them.

No, the Lazy M wouldn't become a cluster of department stores, chain restaurants, gas stations catering to endless yuppies stealing out to the country to pollute the air with the exhaust from their overpriced SUVs.

Had she noticed his limp?

Hell, it shouldn't bother him. He didn't care about impressing Suzanne Hartwell with his manliness. He simply wanted to prove to her she was wrong about what the town needed.

Trying to gather his wits and cool his temper, Rafe led her out into the pasture to show her firsthand one of the many wonders of ranch life—the beauty of horses running in the wild before a natural backdrop of lush green mountains covered with dogwoods and wildflowers. A palomino and a black-and-white paint galloped across the hills, their long manes dancing in the wind. His own black stallion raced behind them at a thunderous pace. Rafe stopped and leaned on the edge of the fencepost, a peacefulness enveloping him as he watched the animals chase across the open space.

"They are beautiful," Suzanne said in a breathy voice that startled him. A voice that was breathy from running to keep up with his gait, not from wanting him, he reminded himself.

He steeled himself against a reaction. "Just got the palomino and the paint in to break. The Stallion's mine. Name's Thunder."

"Figures."

He arched a brow.

"Big man needs a big horse."

He chuckled, but the breeze lifted her hair and tousled it across her face, bringing with it a softer fragrance than the perfume she'd worn the evening before. Must be her daytime perfume.

"I guess you've ridden horses all your life." She smiled up at him, eyes twinkling, as if she was oblivious to the torture she rendered men.

"Since I could walk."

"I wanted a pony when I was small, but my dad said they were too dangerous."

"They are that."

"Dad was slightly overprotective." She leaned her chin on the top of her hands, which were resting on the wooden fence slats. "I always figured it was because my mom wasn't around, but maybe it was his nature."

He cut his gaze toward her, waiting to see if she offered more, remembering how his own father had encouraged him to get right back on that horse after his accident.

"Mom died when I was young." She frowned as she watched the horses. "Cancer."

He shifted on the balls of his feet, wincing at the hint of pain in her voice and ignoring the stab of muscles contracting in his lower left leg. His mother might not be in the best of health, but at least she was alive. Hell if he knew what to say, though. He wasn't good at comfort or talk. "I'm sorry."

Her thin shoulders lifted slightly. "Thanks, but it was a long time ago."

Only, it felt like yesterday, he thought, detecting a hardened edge to her voice. An edge that warned him not to cross the line and pry.

An edge that made him want to.

She was tough, he realized, not the weepy sort. Independent to a fault. Like the horses he tamed.

His admiration for her rose, as well as protective instincts that he had no business feeling.

"My grandfather used to say that a man's job was to protect a woman," he offered. "Guess your father was just doing his job."

Suzanne laughed, a light throaty sound that brushed his nerve endings with desire. "You were born in the wrong time period, Mr. McAllister."

"Why's that?" Irritation sliced through him as he pulled himself up straight. "Because I believe in tradition."

"Because you hold on to the past."

He crossed his arms and glared down at her. "Maybe you let it go too easily."

She righted herself, her height still slight compared to his imposing frame. It didn't seem to faze her. "I look toward the future."

He lowered his voice to a husky whisper, "You fill your life with material things that don't really matter."

"I see the value in change," she whispered in return, "new technology, improved medical techniques."

"You think traffic, smog and kids who are so bored they resort to drugs to entertain themselves are good things?" He made a clicking sound with his teeth. "That's selling out your soul for a buck, Suzanne."

"The advantages override the flaws, Rafe." A spark of anger brightened the inky depths of her eyes, and the sun's golden rays left amber flecks in her hair as she scowled at him. Her spunk sent an undercurrent of awareness zinging through him.

He had thought there was nothing more beautiful than horses running free over the mountainside, nothing more dangerous than a wild one, fighting to run free. He suddenly realized he was wrong.

Suzanne Hartwell was both heartstoppingly beautiful and wild. And far more dangerous.

Doing the only smart thing he could, he turned and walked away from her. "Come on, let me give you your first riding lesson. Once you feel the mare beneath you and experience the heavenly places he can take you, you may change your mind."

SUZANNE ALMOST BARKED a laugh. Rafe was undeniably the most infuriating man she'd ever laid eyes on or attempted to conduct business with.

Although she suspected his comment had nothing to do with business or the future of the town but everything to do with the surge of chemistry crackling between them. What had he meant by feeling the mare beneath her and seeing the heavenly places he could take her? Had she imagined the subtle innuendo beneath his husky promise?

It didn't matter. She would not let this rancher get to her.

She could hold her own with any man, had been doing so for years. And she hadn't made herself a success by bowing down to every macho man who thought women should still be barefoot and pregnant.

Or by letting a man have his way with her.

Perspiration beaded between her breasts. Good Lord, where had that ridiculous thought come from?

Rafe grabbed a rope and wound one end around his hand to form a lasso, then walked slowly toward the stallion. Sensing his game, the horse responded, trotting around the pasture, playing at being caught, Rafe's movements moving in unison with the massive horse's bulk. Was he going to put her on this huge beast? The one he said he usually rode?

Talking in low, hushed tones, he soothed and cajoled, his voice a whispery thread as he coaxed the stallion to him. The horse finally brayed one last time, then settled next to Rafe, allowing him to stroke his back. He slowly slipped the rope around the horse's neck, murmuring soft words of reassurance as he led Thunder across the grass. Suzanne watched, fascinated by the connection between man and beast, at the juxtaposition of the animal's powerful moves and Rafe's confident ones, at their sizes side by side.

"Follow me to the barn. We'll saddle him up and then I'll take you for a ride."

A flutter of nerves attacked Suzanne. "I-I'm not sure I'm experienced enough for him."

The tips of Rafe's long black hair brushed his collar as he angled his face toward her. "Don't worry, sugar. I'll teach you everything you need to know."

Chapter Five

"If you're going to ride, you need to learn how to care for the horse," Rafe said, as he looped the rope around the wooden post near the barn. "Before we saddle him, we always brush and clean him. He'll get sore from the saddle if it's not done properly."

Suzanne shaded her eyes with her hand. "Makes sense."

Rafe retrieved the bucket of brushes, combs and powders from the shed and showed her how to use them, trying to concentrate on the task and not the gentle way Suzanne Hartwell stroked Thunder's crest or the scent of her perfume overriding the smell of fly powder. "Don't ever stand behind the horse or he might kick you."

"Typical male," Suzanne said with a sassy smile.

He pinned her with a dark look. "A man has to defend himself."

Suzanne laughed out loud, a soft musical sound that reminded him of his mother playing the piano. He shook his head as she petted Thunder, crooning nonsensical baby talk to him while she dragged the brush through his mane, telling him what a pretty baby he was. His twenty-hand stallion whinnied and nudged his nose into her hand, falling under her hypnotic spell.

The big traitor.

"All right, now we saddle him up." Rafe spread the saddle blanket over Thunder's back, then reached for the black saddle, explaining his movements as he demonstrated how to fit the bit into the horse's mouth and secure the bridle and saddle straps. "Make sure it's tight enough that it won't slip when you get on."

"Looks easy enough." She reached for the stirrup, but he brushed her aside.

"You need to learn how to do it yourself." He spotted Bud standing in the barn doorway. "Bring Blondie out here for Miss Suzanne."

His sixty-five-year-old hand grinned toothily. "Sure enough."

Rafe almost laughed as surprise registered on Suzanne's face. She was so confident he'd do all the dirty work.

He was supposed to be charming her into his way of thinking, showing her the beauty of the land, not putting her through some willpower test. He'd just have to suck it up, be charming to her and forget this crazy attraction.

Surely he could control himself. After all, he didn't like Suzanne Hartwell. She'd come to his ranch looking like some designer cowgirl ready to pose for a Western-wear catalog. Her jeans were so tight, he was surprised she could breathe, her perfume was so sweet it was damn near nauseating, and she would probably kill herself trying to ride in those stupid high-heeled boots.

She was not the kind of woman who belonged on a ranch.

SUZANNE GRITTED HER TEETH at the sight of the sway-backed mare. Her coat was a dusty beige, her slow gait a sure sign that she had settled into seniorhood. Gracious, the poor thing looked as if she should be resting in the shady barn chewing on an apple instead of saddled up and ridden. Not that this horse would give Suzanne a wild ride. It probably couldn't even work up to a canter.

"Have fun, missy." Bud, the sweet-looking old ranch hand, winked at her as he loped back to the barn.

Suzanne eyed the horse skeptically. "Are you sure she's up to being ridden?"

"You admitted yourself you're not experienced. She's the tamest horse on the Lazy M." His crooked grin plucked at her nerves. "After all, I promised to show you my property. I don't want to get sued in case you fall off."

"Oh, of course." The poor guy was broke. He was worried about being sued.

"Go ahead, let's see what you remember." Rafe gestured toward the bucket of brushes, a brown saddle and striped Mexican blanket in the corner of the shed.

Recognizing the challenge in his eyes, she offered him a perky smile, grabbed the comb and began to clean the pathetic horse. Blondie relaxed under her ministrations, her mellow attitude vastly different from the energy that had emanated from Thunder. Suzanne hummed to herself, trying to ignore the odor of horse dung lingering in the area.

Rafe's manly presence dared her to forget her real business with the studly rancher. But the intensity of his gaze unnerved her, as if part of him wanted to lap her up and the other part wanted to watch her fall flat on her face on the dusty ground and admit that she had been wrong to even suggest progress come to Sugar Hill.

When she was finally satisfied she'd combed enough tangles from the mare's coat, Suzanne spread the blanket over Blondie's middle, grateful the animal didn't balk. Then she tried to lift the saddle and nearly collapsed with its weight.

Rafe had the nerve to grin. "Big horse needs a big saddle."

Suzanne rolled her eyes. "You mean an overweight horse needs a heavy saddle. This thing weighs more than I do," Suzanne said, forgetting she was not supposed to give Rafe a reason to think she was a wimpy city girl. He obviously disagreed with her ideals and life style, and would hate her if he knew she worked for Horton Developers.

She tried the saddle again, wobbling on the heels of her boots and nearly breaking her back, but she finally maneuvered both hands beneath it and lifted it from the floor. Wood boards squeaked beneath her feet, her shoulder muscles strained, and she staggered toward Blondie, nearly diving headfirst into her drooping belly as the weight pulled at her arms. She definitely needed to work out more at the gym and build up her upper body strength.

Steadying herself, she tried to raise her arms and throw the saddle on top of the horse, but one of the straps smacked her in the eye and she wobbled backward, her butt brushing Rafe's thighs.

He caught her, his broad hands encasing her arms, the whisper of his breath against her neck sending a tingle through her. A hiss escaped him as he disengaged her from the front of his body.

"Here, just let me do it." Exasperation laced his voice.

Suzanne shook her head, her stubborn streak rearing its head. "No, I can manage." Pushing his hands away with her elbow, she sucked in a huge breath, stood on tiptoe and heaved the saddle over Blondie's back. Several grunt-filled minutes later, she'd tightened the straps and secured the bit and bridle, pleased with the way Blondie tipped her head for affection.

"All right, are you ready to go?" Rafe asked.

Suzanne nodded, although she was already exhausted from the ordeal. Rafe slung one foot into the stirrup, then mounted Thunder like a professional rodeo star while she struggled to climb in the saddle.

The ring James had given her dug into her finger as she clenched the reins.

Rafe might have won this round, but he would not

win in the end. Suzanne would make sure James got this land, and she'd get the promotion she wanted. It was only a matter of time before Rafe had to admit that she was right, that the best thing he could do for himself and his ailing mother was sell.

She forced her eyes away from his muscular backside so as not to get distracted.

RAFE GLANCED at the fine snakeskin of Suzanne's boots, wondering where she'd found such hideous things and why she thought wearing them to walk through pastures was appropriate. They had to be about the most uncomfortable-looking pair of boots he'd ever laid eyes on. She was a stubborn thing, too. He was sure she would have balked at the idea of riding Blondie. "Keep your heels down, toes up. If you don't and the horse throws you, you'll get caught in the stirrups."

"You mean Blondie throws people?"

He bit back a laugh at the note of panic in her voice. Definitely a city girl, this one.

"No. It's just good riding practice." He tightened Thunder's reins, urging him to fall into a gait the old mare could keep up with as they rode.

"Anything else I should know about?" Suzanne asked.

"Hold the reins in one hand. Squeeze the horse with your thighs and calves," he said. "You ride with your legs, not your whole body like most people think."

He dragged his gaze forward as he saw her visibly

clench her thighs. Lord, this woman conjured up wicked fantasies.

"This is the south pasture," he said, pointing to the cattle grazing nearby. "I rotate them periodically to give the grass time to replenish itself."

Blondie waddled behind him, Suzanne's long dark hair dancing in the wind as they quickened their pace. She didn't talk much as they crossed the tumbling hills and dipped into the valley, the horse's easy gait allowing her to experience the scope of the breathtaking vista. Despite her inexperience, she took naturally to the saddle, her lithe long body graceful as she bounced in rhythm with the horse.

He explained his operation as he guided her down a trail to the east side of his property. Mossy banks flanked the stream that gurgled along the mountainside, eventually flowing into the pond where his cattle drank and found shade from the summer heat.

"Look at those mountains," he said. "The peaks are the first things I see in the morning when I look out my bedroom window. I rode out here and played in the woods all the time when I was a kid."

"They are lovely," Suzanne agreed.

"The dogwoods should be blooming pretty soon," Rafe added. "When they're blooming at once, it looks like a sea of snowflakes."

"We used to have a dogwood in the yard where I lived when I was little," Suzanne said in a voice that suddenly sounded small, as if she was remembering a time that had been lost to her until the sight of the mountainside had resurrected it. "I'd almost forgotten about it."

"Where was that? Atlanta?"

"One of the suburbs. But Dad sold the house for a condo after Mom died."

Rafe hesitated, once again detecting a note of sadness in her voice. "Sounds like you miss it."

"Actually, I haven't thought about it in years. The condo was nice. We had a pool and there was always stuff to do. Dad entertained a lot, too."

"Backyard barbecues for your friends?"

She glanced at him, a small pinched look forming between her eyes. "Not really. Mostly his business clients."

"Sounds like loads of fun."

She frowned. "It was all right."

"No trees at the condo, though?"

"One or two."

"Wedged in the cement for looks, huh?"

Her silence verified the answer.

"I bet you didn't have pets, either."

"They weren't allowed." She shrugged. "Besides, Rebecca got so upset when the neighbor's goldfish died, Dad didn't want her getting attached to anything else."

"What about you?" He arched a brow, guiding Thunder around a bend by the creek until they'd found one of his favorite spots, a clearing nestled in a cluster of trees. The grass sprouted wildflowers that dotted the ground with purple and yellow. A huge oak offered a sanctuary from the sun, its drooping branches shrouded with Spanish moss.

"What do you mean?"

"Didn't you ever want a dog or a cat? Something to romp and play with in the yard."

Suzanne shrugged. "I guess I never gave it much thought. Dad was so busy with work and…and we had activities." She sighed and patted Blondie's mane. "Besides, we moved around a lot."

No place to call home. He let the silence lapse between them. He couldn't imagine not having peace and quiet, the animals, the woods and trees and open spaces to run free. Had she been happy moving all over the place?

He had not brought her here to get to know her or wonder if she was happy, he reminded himself; he wanted her to understand the significance of his ranch to him.

The importance of preserving family memories and landscapes. Except he wanted to forget a few things…like his father's betrayal.

Bitterness filled him at the thought of having to clean up the mess his father had left behind. And worse, having to lie to his mother.

It was a damn good thing that developer didn't know about his money problems. He might try to use that weak spot against him.

A TWINGE OF UNEASE needled Suzanne at the questions Rafe had asked her, but she didn't understand why. She'd never questioned the fact that she might have missed something growing up. She'd simply adapted, used her time with her father to help him out, playing hostess to his parties. She'd learned to do all the girl things girls did, like shopping and makeup and, of course, boys. Sports had taken up time, as well.

She hadn't cared if she'd had a yard or a tree to climb or a dog. Then again, a faint memory surfaced. When she was little, shortly after her mother died, she'd hugged her stuffed kitty and wished he was real. Because she'd missed her mother.

"You let things go too easily," Rafe had said.

Had she let her mother go too easily?

No, she'd simply grown tough to survive.

Rafe steered the horses to a shady place to graze, then dismounted, and she did the same, pushing the troubling thoughts away. They let the horses drink from the creek while Rafe regaled her with stories of ranch life. The cattle rides when he'd been young, the overnight camping trips where he slept beneath the stars and moon, the old-fashioned picnics and parades in the town. "The people in Sugar Hill care about each other. They may not be rich, but they still believe in helping out their neighbor." He removed his Stetson, and ran his long, tanned fingers through his dark locks. "I bet you can't say that where you live."

Actually, she'd never even met her neighbors. "You've never wanted to travel, to see different parts of the world?"

He shrugged. "Sure. Maybe one day I will." His

gaze slid across the lush countryside. "But my heart would always be here."

"What about your mother? Wouldn't you like to find a nice new house for her, someplace that would offer assistance for her as she ages?"

"I would never put my mother in a home," he said in a thunderous voice. "The McAllisters take care of their own." He stood and brushed grass from his jeans. "Besides, my mother loves this place as much as I do. A rancher's land is his pride. If he loses that, what's left?"

Suzanne studied the intense look in his eyes, the rigid set to his mouth and broad shoulders, and saw a man filled with conviction. Admiration mushroomed inside her, although she had to remind herself he was the enemy.

He tucked his hat back on his head, his gaze piercing her. "We'd best get back now. I still have half a day's work to do."

Suzanne nodded, struggling over how to reply. She had work to do, too, but all of it involved convincing him to sell, looking over the plans for the development and design, and composing arguments to counteract any protest the town members might have.

And if what he said was true, if his land was his pride, if he really thought he'd have nothing left if he lost the ranch, she would be calculating how she planned to take it all away from him.

Chapter Six

"Come back tomorrow and I'll show you some other sights on the property," Rafe said as they brushed the horses after dismounting at the barn.

"Sure." Suzanne patted Blondie's back. "I enjoyed the ride."

"You're a natural." She would probably be a natural at other things, too. He put the supplies away, then washed his hands, trying to cleanse himself of his lustful thoughts. But their fingers touched briefly, a frisson of awareness rippling through him. The same kind of longing he'd felt by the pond when she'd stretched out those long legs and he'd imagined them wrapped around his waist.

That was the reason he'd abruptly decided they had to return to the ranch. The clearing by the pond was too secluded, too tempting. Back at the barn, there was safety in numbers.

Besides, he had work to do, and no time to flirt with Suzanne Hartwell.

He dried his hands, waited until she'd done the

same, then gestured for her to lead. He'd follow her to her car, then put her out of his mind. At least until tomorrow.

But as he crossed the yard, he spotted his mother holding on to her walker, clipping the rosebushes along the trellis, and he took off at a jog. Seconds later he stood beside her, gazing at her weathered features, her pale complexion. "What are you doing out here, Mom? I thought you were supposed to be resting."

Suzanne appeared beside him, looking flushed, windblown and concerned.

His mother chuckled, pushing a loose thread of gray hair beneath her straw hat. "Honey, I have to tend the flowers. I can't stay holed up all the time or I'll go plumb nuts."

Rafe's heart was still pounding irregularly. "I know, but you should wait until I'm here or one of the hands are nearby. What if you fell?"

"I'd call for Maria. She's out back hanging the sheets on the line to dry." She hesitated, straightening her hat, and peered from him to Suzanne. "Aren't you going to introduce me to your friend, Rafe? You didn't tell me we had company or I'd have changed."

"She's..." A friend, he started to say, then caught himself.

"I'm Suzanne Hartwell." Suzanne extended her right hand, her big sapphire ring shimmering. "And you look fine, Mrs. McAllister. I just came out for a riding lesson."

"Oh, yes." Rafe's mother flattened a hand over her housedress. "Rafe said he'd decided to teach. He's such a good rider. I hope he showed you the lovely pond."

Rafe frowned, determined to get rid of Suzanne before his mother got any matchmaking ideas in her head. The wheels were obviously spinning already.

"Yes, it was beautiful. And so are your roses." Suzanne's smile seemed genuine. "My Grammy Rose adores her flower garden, too. She has this lovely gazebo draped with roses that overlook Pine Mountain."

"It sounds like a postcard," Rafe's mother exclaimed. "Or a lovely place for a wedding." She gave Rafe a pointed look, which he ignored, silently praying Suzanne hadn't detected the hint. Lately, his mother had been badgering him about wanting grandchildren.

Like he could afford another mouth to feed right now.

"As a matter of fact, my cousins and sisters got married there."

Mrs. McAllister's gaze dropped to Suzanne's ring. "Oh, are you engaged yourself, dear?"

The ring tightened around her finger. "No. Sapphire is my birthstone." She hated to lie to the sweet woman, but she wasn't officially engaged.

Rafe barely managed not to grunt. "Well, ladies, I have to get back to work. Mom, can I help you inside?"

"Certainly. Why don't you join me, Suzanne? I'll

have Maria bring us some sweet tea. I believe she baked some homemade lemon-drop cookies this morning, too. You want to have some with us, Rafe? You look awfully hot and sweaty.''

"No tea for me, too much work to do. I'm sure Suzanne has other stuff to do, too—"

"Tea and cookies sound fabulous," Suzanne said, surprising Rafe. "I'd love to visit a while."

Rafe frowned. She would? "Don't you have to get back to Atlanta?" he asked, more bluntly than he'd realized because his mother threw him one of her reprimanding glares.

"I'm not in a hurry." Suzanne took his mother's arm and helped her up the creaking porch steps.

"We can carry them out back to the screened porch," his mother said, her voice gaining excitement. "It's nice and cool there this time of day. And I have a bird feeder out back and this lovely nest of baby sparrows we can watch."

Rafe bit the inside of his cheek to keep from screaming. He did not want Suzanne to stay and visit with his mother or tempt him to shirk his work and eat lemon-drop cookies in the shade. And, damn it, he *was* tempted.

Suzanne's backside swayed as she ascended the stairs in her tight jeans. He definitely didn't want her cozying up to his mother and have her fabricate some crazy romantic notions that she would harp on for the next week. "I just thought Suzanne might be in a hurry to leave today. She's not much of a farm girl."

"Rafe McAllister, don't be rude to our guest," his mother said. "You know how much I love company." She turned to Suzanne. "Poor boy hasn't had any women around in so long, I guess he's forgotten how to behave."

"I wasn't being rude, I thought she might have a date or something."

"No, no date," Suzanne offered.

He could have sworn her eyes were laughing, and wondered why he had made that inane comment.

"So, no date," his mother said with a triumphant smile, as if she'd thought Rafe was fishing for information. "See, Rafe, she can stay."

"But I can't." He backed away, almost stumbling over the rocking chair on the front porch in his haste to escape her.

"I understand perfectly." Suzanne's eyes twinkled. "I certainly don't want to bother you, either."

He gestured toward her little sporty car. "I thought you might be visiting your family while you were here, Suzanne."

"Actually I am. I'm staying at Rebecca's old apartment, right down from the bookstore."

His mother hooted as if she'd just realized the connection. "Oh, mercy, you're related to Wiley Hartwell, aren't you?"

Suzanne blushed. "He's my uncle. Hannah, Mimi and Alison are my cousins, and my sister is Rebecca."

"They are lovely girls. And that Wiley, he is such a character." She pushed her walker slowly ahead into the foyer. "We were downright lucky he was giving that pickup truck away for New Year's. Things have been mighty tight around here, and your uncle saved Rafe—"

"Mother," Rafe practically ground out the word. "I doubt Suzanne is interested in our family problems."

Suzanne's expressive eyes found his, a flicker of emotion darkening the depths as if he was wrong. As if she might be personally interested in his life.

In him.

Then the moment passed, and he realized he'd misread her. There was nothing between them but a little heat and the matter of their opposing opinions over the future of Sugar Hill. So he offered a clipped goodbye and strode down the steps to finish his day while his mother and Suzanne enjoyed their tea party. Maybe Maria's cookies would be hard as bricks and Suzanne would chip a tooth on them and never come back.

Then he wouldn't be tortured by her presence.

"SEE THAT MAGNOLIA out there," Mrs. McAllister pointed to the right side of the porch. "Frank and I planted that tree when Rafe was born. His birthday's in April, right when the flowers bloom." She laid a hand over her stomach. "We wanted more children, but it didn't work out. But Rafe has been the best son a mother could want. He works night and day to keep this place going."

Suzanne sipped the sweet iced tea and reached for

another cookie. "You've never thought of moving someplace where he wouldn't have to work so hard?"

Mrs. McAllister laughed. "That boy grew up here, ranching's in his blood. He wouldn't know how to do anything else." She dusted powdered sugar from her dress. "God rest his soul, my husband sure didn't know anything else, either. Some men are just born to live off the land."

Suzanne grew quiet, studying the green leaves on the magnolia tree. Another month and the white flowers would bloom, celebrating another year for the tree and honoring Rafe's birthday.

The same month the developer for the mall project wanted to break ground.

"Those tulip buds out there remind me of my mother," Mrs. McAllister said softly. "Lordy, she loved tulips. And that oak tree by the pond, why that was where Frank and I said our vows. We didn't have a fancy wedding, just family, but I can still see him standing under that tree wearing his suit and tie." She swiped at a tear pooling in the corner of her eye. "Sometimes when I sit out here in the evenings, I can hear his voice whispering to me through the pines." She gave Suzanne a beseeching look. "It's almost as if he's still here. Every time I smell Old Spice, I break down and cry."

Suzanne nodded. She had tried so hard *not* to think about her mother, not to miss her, to be strong and move on, that she had never really felt her presence. Emotions converged inside her, though, and she fingered the cross dangling between her breasts, remembering the sadness in her mother's eyes as she'd handed it to her on her deathbed.

She tried to remember her mother's face, to see her eyes and hear her voice. To remember the perfume she'd worn.

Instead, she envisioned that awful metal hospital bed that sat like a big claw holding her mother's emaciated frame in the dark corner of the den. She smelled the scent of alcohol and antiseptic and fear that had nearly choked her when she'd entered the room. She heard the wheezing sound of the oxygen mask when her mother had gathered pain-filled, frightening breaths. And the drip of that IV—she used to wake up sweating, dreaming about that sound.

Maybe that was the reason her father had sold their house so soon after her mother had died. So he wouldn't see her mother everywhere he turned, so he wouldn't hear her voice whispering to him at night or hear that haunting drip. So he wouldn't have to look at the place where that horrid hospital bed had sat, the place where her mother had died.

"Well, it's so good to have you visit," Mrs. McAllister said, drawing her from her reverie. "I think we're going to be good friends."

Suzanne smiled and squeezed her hand, guilt suffusing her. She would like that, she thought. Except the kind, old woman might not like her so much if she knew the real reason Suzanne had come to the Lazy M.

RAFE HAD WORKED all afternoon replacing rotten fencing out on the edge of the west pasture, ham-

mering and digging post holes, grateful for the physical labor to work off his tension. While his mind
zigzagged from thoughts of Suzanne Hartwell to the
committee that had been formed to explore the pros
and cons of the new development proposed for the
town, he struggled for other ways to increase his in-
come. Hopefully, he'd take in some horses to board
soon. And if worse came to worst, he'd agree to lease
some of his property to his neighbor, Harold Landon,
who'd been wanting to increase his herd for the past
year, although that would be a last resort. He didn't
like Landon or his methods of breeding, and despised
the fact that his father had owed him money. The
fact that Landon knew Rafe was in financial trouble
made things worse. The developer hounding him was
bad enough, but Landon had offered several times to
buy the Lazy M.

It would be a cold day in July before Rafe sold
his land to Harold Landon.

Rafe finished stacking the supplies, then loaded the
extras in the back of that gaudy purple pickup truck
and headed back to the farmhouse for dinner. His
stomach growled, a reminder he'd skipped lunch. He
only hoped Maria's cooking was better than her laundry skills.

Surely Suzanne Hartwell was gone by now.

But as he drove up, he saw her walking toward
her convertible, a smile on her face as she waved to
his mother. His mother looked refreshed and pleased
as punch.

Why was Suzanne Hartwell getting all chummy with his mother?

"Hi, Rafe."

"Hey." He glanced at his mother who was overflowing with good spirits, then glared at Suzanne. "I didn't expect you to still be here."

"I guess the day got away from me."

"I invited her to stay for supper, but she said she's meeting her sister," his mother called. "We had the nicest visit, Rafe. Did you know Suzanne can cook? She told me about this chocolate layer cake, and I just have to try it."

Oh, great, he was in big trouble now. According to his mother, anyone who had half a brain in the kitchen was wife material. Although he was surprised Suzanne could cook; he'd pegged her as more of the eat-out type.

"And I showed her how to crochet. She's never done it before."

Suzanne Hartwell crocheting? "Glad you two had a nice visit." He strode past Suzanne, ignoring the way his body hardened at the mere sight of those dark eyes raking over him. She'd probably never seen a man come home filthy and sweaty and covered in dust from a hard day's work.

"Thanks for the tea and cookies, and for showing me those basic crochet stitches," Suzanne said.

"It was my pleasure, dear. Come back to see us," his mother chirped. "You're welcome anytime."

"Actually, I have another riding lesson tomorrow, so I guess I'll see you then."

Oh, Lord. He'd forgotten about that.

She offered him a smile, and he tipped his head down toward her, his Stetson riding low on his head. "Yeah, tomorrow we'll finish what we started today."

She arched a brow, and he realized she might have mistaken his words.

"By the end of the week, you'll see things my way," he said to clarify his meaning. "Then you'll jump on the bandwagon in town and help us get rid of that developer."

A small frown twitched at her forehead, but she smiled and climbed into her sports car. "We'll see," she said, then waved goodbye.

He glared at the car as it barreled down the drive. Old mistrusts rose like a hawk breathing down his neck. Cecilia had seemed nice, too. She'd even played up to his mother. But she'd set him up to make her rich boyfriend jealous, and Rafe had suffered one of the worst beatings of his life when her little act had worked.

He'd learned a very good but painful lesson that day.

Suzanne Hartwell did not seem like the type to sit at home and entertain his mother. And he certainly couldn't imagine her crocheting sweaters or baking cookies.

Just what was she up to?

TOMORROW WE'LL FINISH what we started today.

The evening breeze caressed Suzanne's face as she

drove toward town. For a minute she had thought
Rafe was implying something else. But she should
have realized he hadn't. Although she detected that
spark of desire in his eyes when he'd spotted her.

So, why had he acted so cool, so detached, as if
he resented the fact that she'd stayed and befriended
his mother?

She parked in front of Rebecca's former apartment, grateful her sister hadn't leased it to anyone
else yet, so she wouldn't have to drive back to the
city tonight. Before she met Rebecca for dinner, she
desperately needed a shower and a change of clothes.
She smelled like horses and hay. It reminded her of
Rafe.

What was he doing right now? Would he eat dinner with his mother, then head to the Dusty Pub?
Would he meet up with another woman and spend
the night in her arms?

The thought irked her, although she knew she had
no right.

She climbed the stairs to the apartment and let
herself in, thinking of Rebecca and how happy she
seemed now. How she would be crawling into bed
in her new house with her new husband tonight.

How she herself would be sleeping alone.

Envy skated through Suzanne. Then she glanced
at the sapphire ring on her finger and her stomach
knotted. What was she going to tell James? Did she
want to marry him and spend every day by his side
and every night in his arms?

From the bedroom, the hope chest drew her eye. She'd almost forgotten about it, but she'd left it here after Rebecca's wedding because it wouldn't fit in her car. The top of the trunk lay open and she spotted the lacy pair of Western boots, that lace choker, and the bridal hat that reminded her of a Stetson. And those knitting needles....

An odd feeling zinged through her, and she glanced down at the cowboy boots. No, those items did not have any significance. She was not meant to be a cowboy's bride.

Suddenly the telephone rang. She glanced at the caller ID and frowned. The ring tightened on her finger.

It was James. Did he want an answer to his proposal?

Chapter Seven

Suzanne let the machine take the message. "Hey, this is James. Just wondering how it went with McAllister today. I'm sure you have him wrapped around your finger by now, ready to sell. Oh, and I have some more information on his family, it's about his father, some pretty shady stuff. If things get desperate, we might be able to use it. Call me."

She stared at the handset. Did she really want to know the information he had on Rafe's family? Something shady about his father?

Did Rafe know whatever it was James had uncovered?

That's the tree where Frank and I said our vows, Rafe's mother had said. *I can still hear his voice whispering to me through the pines at night.*

Suzanne shivered. Had Rafe's mother known the shady things her husband had done and loved him anyway? If they used the info, would Suzanne wind up hurting the frail old woman and Rafe by shattering their loving memories?

Confused, she headed to the shower to wash off the smell of the horses and the feeling of deceit that lingered on her skin from cozying up to his mother.

But she hadn't been playing up to Mrs. McAllister. She had really enjoyed the older woman's company. The conversation, the tranquility of the screened porch, even the crocheting lessons.

Which scared her even more.

She had realized how much she'd missed her own mother. She thought about the afternoons they might have spent shopping, the photos her mother would have taken as she'd dressed for her first dance, the selection of her first prom dress together. Maybe she'd have taught her to sew.

How would her life have been different if her mother hadn't died when Suzanne was so young? What advice would she have given her about boyfriends? Would she have shared stories about how she and her father had met? Told her all the things he'd refused to talk about…?

Now that she'd gotten to know Rafe's mother, could Suzanne reveal some family secret that might hurt her?

RAFE SPENT ALL DINNER listening to his mother rave over her visit with Suzanne.

"She is the sweetest thing I ever met, and pretty, too. Don't you think she's pretty, Rafe?"

He harrumphed and tore his biscuit in two, spreading butter in between the flaky pieces.

"Well, you are blind, son, if you didn't notice.

And she can cook. Some girls these days are so spoiled they can't boil water. Every woman needs to know her way around a kitchen." She scooped a spoonful of gravy on her mashed potatoes. "After all, the way to a man's heart is through his stomach. Girls these days forget that."

"That's because they're more interested in their careers than being wives," Rafe pointed out.

"Some women can juggle both, though, don't you think?"

"I guess."

"I reckon we have to get with the times, son, although, I would like for you to find some nice girl who wouldn't mind taking a vacation from her career to have a family."

Oh, Lord, more grandchildren talk.

"I'd like to hold my grandbaby in my arms before my eyes completely go."

His throat caught. "Is there something wrong with your eyes, Mother?"

She waved her linen napkin at him. "Oh, heavens no, but you know what I mean. I don't want to be too old to play with the little tyke."

"I hate to disappoint you, but I have no intention of getting married anytime soon."

"I realize you've been working too hard to court a woman the right way, but sometimes love happens when you least expect it."

"I'm not interested," he stated baldly, hoping to end the discussion.

"Oh, psshaw. You're a red-blooded male. You

can't tell me you didn't think about asking that pretty Suzanne out.''

He hadn't thought about it because it was a ridiculous idea. ''No, I didn't. She is not my type at all, Mother.''

''Not your type?'' She perched her fork in midair, a butterbean on the tip of the prongs, while she studied him. ''Why isn't she your type? She's female.''

''I don't chase everything in a skirt.''

''Well, you used to.''

His fingers tightened around the fork. ''I've grown up.''

She popped the bean in her mouth, then sipped her sweet tea, her color looking much brighter tonight than it had this morning. He should be grateful Suzanne's visit had perked her up. ''Is Suzanne too skinny for you? Some men like curvy women, but I thought you liked skinny ones. That Cecilia was skinny.''

Grind salt into his wounds by reminding him of Cecilia. ''No, of course she's not too thin.'' His hands could just span Suzanne's waist.

''You don't like dark eyes?''

''Her eyes are fine.''

''Fine? They're gorgeous. I've never seen eyes so dark.''

''All right, they're gorgeous.''

''Then she's too tall for you?''

''No, she's not too tall.'' Her legs were just right, long and graceful....

''See, she's perfect. A big man like you doesn't

need some teeny little thing that would have to step on a ladder to kiss him.''

"Mother." Rafe scrubbed his hand over his face. He did not feel comfortable discussing any of this with his mother. "I'm not interested in kissing her."

"You're not?"

He wanted to do a lot more than that with her, but he couldn't very well tell his mother that. "No!"

The ice in her glass clinked as she sat it down. "Rafe, are you sick or something?"

"No. Just stop with the matchmaking, okay?"

She frowned and sighed, frowned and sighed. "I don't understand. Why are you getting so touchy? A beautiful single woman comes here for riding lessons, and you take her out for the day and she's coming back again, and she's from a decent family, she's educated—"

Exactly. Too damn educated and rich for him. "I told you…she's not my type."

"You have a girlfriend already?"

"Of course not. But in case you didn't notice, Suzanne Hartwell has city gal written all over her." He wolfed down his tea, spilling it on the front of his shirt in his haste to finish dinner and this ghastly inquisition. "Did you see that ridiculous outfit and gaudy ring she had on? She lives in Atlanta. She knows nothing about life on a ranch." He stood, grabbed an extra biscuit, determined to escape. "Now, I'm going to look over the books and see if I can come up with some way to save our home."

"She's coming back tomorrow," his mother said

over her shoulder, as if she'd seen through his act. "So you'd better be nice to her, Rafe."

Oh, he'd be nice. Just enough to convince her to stop encouraging the mall project. But he'd keep his hands to himself, and his heart under armored padlock.

"So, HOW DID IT GO with Rafe McAllister?" Rebecca asked.

Suzanne frowned into her lemonade. They had met at a new diner in Sugar Hill called Dilly's and ordered salads and pasta. Their cousins were due any minute, too. Apparently, the women had decided to have ladies' night out once a week, and since Suzanne was in town, she had been included.

It was both strange and nice to be part of a girls' group. Suzanne had been so busy with her job the past couple of years, she hadn't made any close friends in Atlanta. Other than James.

She still hadn't called him back.

"Earth to Suzanne," Rebecca said. "Was he difficult?"

No, she wouldn't describe Rafe as difficult. Although it had been difficult not to stare at him. "Well, not really."

"He knows you work for Horton Developers?"

Suzanne winced. "Not quite."

Rebecca chewed her lip. "You mean you lied to him?"

"Not exactly. I told him I worked in an office and raise money for charities."

Rebecca's frown spoke volumes. "Did you talk about selling his land?"

Suzanne traced a droplet of water running down her glass. "We discussed the town meeting, so he knows I'm in favor of the development. He dared me to come out and see his property and then decide."

"He thinks you'll fall in love with it and see it his way."

Suzanne nodded. "That's his plan."

"And what's yours?"

Suzanne hesitated and Rebecca gasped.

"You aren't going to seduce him into selling, are you?"

"No!" Suzanne screeched. "Is that really the kind of girl you think I am, Bec?"

Rebecca covered Suzanne's hand with her own. "I didn't mean to offend you, Suzanne. You're charming, you're ambitious and successful, and you came here to do a job." She grinned. "And he is kind of cute."

Suzanne rolled her eyes. "In that rugged, macho, infuriating cowboy kind of way."

"But not your type, huh?"

"No, definitely not." So, why had she thought of nothing but him and his mother after she'd left the Lazy M? Why had she craved his touch when they'd ridden out by the mountains? Why had she wanted him to kiss her in that clearing? Why had it bothered her so much that he didn't like her?

Why had she avoided talking to James?

"So, he showed you his property?"

"Yes, and he gave me a riding lesson. I'm supposed to go riding again tomorrow and do some more sight-seeing."

Rebecca grinned as if she'd read more into the sentence than Suzanne intended, but her cousins arrived in a flurry of excited hugs and hellos, and her protests died as the girls ordered, all chattering at once about how good it was to be together.

"Tonight is wonderful," Mimi said. "I love little Maggie Rose and married life, but a woman needs girl talk, too."

"Me, too," Hannah said. "Although with the baby on the way and my work schedule, I'll have to call it an early night."

"Pregnancy is draining, isn't it?" Mimi said sympathetically.

Hannah patted her burgeoning belly. "Yes, but it's worth it."

"Any news on your side, Alison? Rebecca?" Mimi asked.

Alison and Rebecca traded sheepish grins. "Nothing to report yet," Alison said.

"It's too early to tell," Rebecca said. "We're still newlyweds."

They chatted about the joys of marital life for a few minutes, each joking about the tiny, irritating habits they'd noticed about their new husbands. "Seth is so sweet with the baby," Mimi said, "but I swear, I still have to remind him to be spontaneous sometimes."

Everyone laughed. "And I have to remind Brady not to be too serious," Alison said.

"Thankfully, Jake's finally getting accustomed to our big family. It was odd for him at first."

Suzanne could relate. She'd always felt isolated for some reason. Although her father had doted on her and she adored Rebecca, the three of them had never overcome the loss of her mother. And then her father had hopped from one wife to another.

"All right," Mimi said when their conversation hit a lull. "You know we're all dying to know what Grammy put in your hope chest, Suzanne."

"Yes, tell us," Rebecca coached.

Alison and Hannah piped in, begging, as well. "Tell me about yours first," Suzanne said in an effort to sidetrack them.

Hannah began. "I received Grammy's ring, the one that had the legend saying that if I wore it to bed the night before my wedding I would dream about my future husband," Hannah said.

"And you dreamed about Jake?" Rebecca asked.

"Yes, but I was engaged to Seth."

"So, lucky for me, they broke up," Mimi jumped in dramatically. "And when they got married, Seth offered me a ride home from Grammy's. But it was snowing, and we got stranded in this little B and B, and well, things got out of control, and we sort of lost count of the condoms."

"Grammy put condoms in your hope chest?" Suzanne asked.

The girls laughed. "No, if she had, we might not

have Maggie Rose,'' Mimi said with a laugh. ''I got baby items in my hope chest. Believe me, it was a shock since I thought I wasn't mother material. But it all worked out, and I just love being a mom.''

''What about you, Alison?'' Suzanne asked.

''The annulment papers for my marriage to Brady. See, Brady and I got married the night before he was supposed to leave for the Air Force. But Daddy found out and was furious. Brady and I thought he'd annulled the marriage. Over the years, we drifted apart.'' She squeezed lemon into her tea and took a sip. ''Later, Brady lost his best friend in a helicopter crash and was injured himself. He came home to recuperate. Thomas had just proposed to me, and I didn't know what to do, but when I saw Brady and found out we were still married…well, I still loved Brady.''

''So Thomas was free, then?'' Suzanne said.

Rebecca giggled. ''Yes, and then Grammy gave me my hope chest and it had this book of erotic poetry Grammy had written—''

''Grammy wrote erotic poetry?'' Suzanne was stunned.

Rebecca nodded. ''But my hope chest also had children's books in it, so I started thinking about having a baby, and came up with this baby plan.''

''You were going to ask Thomas to father the baby, weren't you?'' Mimi asked.

''At first, but then I crashed into his car, and he asked me to paint murals on the clinic walls, and we got to know each other…'' She let the sentence trail off.

"And you fell in love," Alison added. "Which was perfect. I'm so glad you found each other."

Rebecca squeezed Alison's hand and they all beamed like proud new wives.

"Now, it's your turn," Rebecca said. "What did Grammy give you, sis?"

Suzanne's stomach had started churning as the girls' stories had unfolded. None of them had been expecting to marry the man they'd wound up with. In fact, all of the things they'd received in their hope chests had somehow been related to their present husbands. And all of them had seemed mismatched at first.

A bad premonition hit her.

"Suzanne?" Mimi said. "What's wrong?"

Suzanne gulped down the lemonade, nearly choking on a seed. "Nothing, it's just that…"

"Just what? What was in your hope chest?" Hannah asked.

She cleared her throat, her voice a mere croak. "A pair of Western-style lacy boots, a lacy Western bridal hat and a choker."

Rebecca's gaze locked with Suzanne's. "Oh, my."

"What?" Mimi, Hannah and Alison all asked at once.

"It isn't true," Suzanne said. "Grammy Rose made a mistake this time."

Rebecca pressed a hand to her lips and grinned.

"Tell us!" Mimi screeched.

"Suzanne just spent the day with Rafe McAllister on his ranch." Rebecca paused dramatically, letting the sentence sink in. "He's teaching her to ride and showing her around his property."

"I bet that's not all he's going to show you," Mimi said.

"I have a feeling you've met your man," Hannah added.

"I might as well get things ready in the bridal shop to start planning another Hartwell wedding," Alison said.

Suzanne shook her head in denial. "We barely know each other. I'm not sure we even like each other."

"Uh-huh," Mimi said. "I didn't think Seth was for me at first."

"I didn't think Thomas liked me either," Rebecca said.

"And Jake thought I might be involved with an illegal car theft ring," Hannah added.

"Brady thought we weren't meant to be together," Alison said.

But that was different, Suzanne thought. And they wouldn't think about marriage if they knew the truth about why she was spending time with Rafe.

And what about James?

As if her sister had read Suzanne's mind, Rebecca gestured toward the sapphire ring. "Have you answered James's proposal yet?"

Suzanne shook her head. "I-I'm not sure what to say to him."

Rebecca gave her a sympathetic look. "Do you love him, Suzanne?"

Suzanne pressed a finger to her temple where a headache was beginning to pulse. Did she love James? She wasn't exactly sure how she felt about him. He certainly didn't send her senses into a dizzying spin like the sight of Rafe....

Chapter Eight

Rafe spent a miserable, sleepless night stewing over the ranch's problems. His morning didn't fare much better. He'd risen at dawn to do three hours of work before he drove his mother into town to the doctor. Thankfully, Hannah Hartwell Tippins had consulted with his mother's rheumatologist so she could treat his mother without a trip to Atlanta each time she needed follow-up treatment. Of course, there were the occasional times when she needed more extensive tests and they had to make the long trek to the city, but for now her condition had stabilized, meaning her medication was working. Her spirits seemed high, too, especially since that visit with Suzanne.

But why had Hannah given him an odd look when he'd left? As if she knew some kind of secret about him that she thought funny.

He must have imagined it, he thought, as he hurried into the grocery store to fill his mother's prescription. He'd left her at the bookstore to browse through the magazines and books, knowing she needed to pick out a few new paperbacks to entertain her while she rested. Dropping the prescription off at the pharmacist's window, he gathered some pain-killers, ointment, cotton balls, milk and bread, tossed in a box of her favorite bubble bath along with some fresh strawberries, then headed to the pharmacist window. But as he rounded the corner near the baby aisle, he nearly crashed into Mimi Hartwell Broad-hurst, carrying a pink bundle.

"Hi, Rafe."

"Hi." He didn't realize Mimi even knew his name.

"I hear you're giving Suzanne riding lessons."

"Yeah."

Mimi grinned, jiggling her daughter up and down on her shoulder. "She told us what a good time she had at your ranch yesterday."

"She did?"

"Yes. You're really sweet to teach her to ride."

Sweet? No one had ever accused him of that before.

"She's a good athlete," Mimi said. "I bet she takes to the saddle pretty easily."

He nodded. She had been a natural. Those long legs and all.... "I'm only doing it so she'll change her mind about supporting that mall project," he said, not knowing why he felt the need to clarify his actions, but Mimi was looking at him oddly, her eyes twinkling just as Hannah's had.

"Oh, right." Mimi winked at him, then walked away, laughing.

What was it with women? First his mother pushing him toward Suzanne, now Mimi Hartwell grinning like he had ulterior motives in giving a riding lesson. Even Hannah, who seemed like the practical sort, had behaved oddly.

What exactly had Suzanne said about him?

"WHAT DID HE SAY about me?" Suzanne asked, studying Rafe's sexy backside as he exited the store.

Mimi grinned. "Just that he was only giving you riding lessons to convince you not to support that mall project. Of course, you know the old saying, 'Me thinks he doth protest too much.'"

"I'm sure he meant what he said," Suzanne said. "For some reason I don't think he likes me."

"What's not to like?" Mimi said, wide-eyed. "He's a man and you're a positively scrumptious woman. He'd be crazy not to be attracted to you. I don't know why you didn't go over and just talk to him. I never thought of you as being shy, Suzanne."

"It's not that," Suzanne said. "But I don't want him to think I'm stalking him." She adjusted her purse on her shoulder. "Besides, I'm buying ingredients to make a cake, and I didn't want him to see me with this recipe book."

"I didn't know you could cook."

Another tiny tidbit she'd sort of fudged yesterday. "I can't. At least not much. But yesterday I told Rafe's mother about this wonderful chocolate cake, and somehow she got the impression that I baked it myself. I guess I forgot to mention that it was our third housekeeper, Mrs. Atkinson, that actually cooked the darn thing.''

Mimi's mouth twitched. ''Uh-huh. You wanted to impress Rafe's mother?''

''I...I guess so.'' Although she had no idea why impressing Mrs. McAllister had seemed important, but it had at the time, so she simply hadn't corrected her assumption. Now, she'd dug herself into a hole. But it wasn't like it was a big lie, really, and what could it hurt to make a sweet, sick woman a cake? Rafe's mother had been so cordial yesterday, so full of Southern hospitality. Besides, Suzanne needed to learn to cook sometime, so why not practice her culinary skills while she had a few days to relax in Sugar Hill? How hard could it be to make a cake? All she had to do was follow the directions.

''Well, keep me posted,'' Mimi said. ''We'll see you at the next town meeting.''

Suzanne nodded and raced through the store to gather the ingredients listed in the recipe, battling nerves. She could handle major mergers and acquisitions, entertain the wealthiest entrepreneurs and close million-dollar deals. Baking a cake should be easy. After all, she'd certainly *served* plenty of cake at receptions before.

She read the ingredients. What exactly was cake flour? Perplexed, she scoured the shelves and discovered more varieties and name brands than she could ever have imagined. Wheat flour, white flour, self-rising flour, all-purpose flour. What in heaven's name was the difference between them and which one was she supposed to buy?

A frown pulled at her mouth. And what in the world was a sifter?

HIS NERVES STRUNG TIGHT, Rafe strode into the bank. Though Slim Wallace had turned down his loan, he hoped he'd cut him some slack on the second mortgage payment. A few minutes later he paced across Wallace's office, his hands jammed in his pockets to keep from pounding the man's snotty face into the stack of papers on his desk marked Past Due—all bills of Rafe's, thanks to his irresponsible father.

"Look, Wallace, it's barely turning spring. Just give me a few more weeks, and I'll have part of the money. I have some beef cattle I'm about ready to sell—"

"I've heard it all before," Wallace said. "From your father and now you." Wallace stood, hands planted on his desk. "Listen, Rafe, I feel for you, I honestly do. But you're in way over your head. You're so far past due that I'm not going to have a choice soon. I'll have to collect or foreclose."

God, no.

Sweat beaded on Rafe's forehead. "You can't do that, Slim. This land has been in my family for generations. It would kill my mother to have to leave her home."

Wallace sighed, twisting a cigar end with his fingers. "Maybe you should tell her the truth. She might be stronger than you think."

"No." He fisted his hands by his side. "Don't you tell her, either. She hasn't been in the best of health, and I don't want to add to it by heaping more stress on her."

"Think about selling part of your land to Landon, then. He's been after it for years."

"He's part of the reason my father got in so much trouble."

"Well, your only other option is to sell to that developer."

Anger mounted in Rafe's chest. "I won't let the Lazy M become another shopping mall."

"Then consider Landon," Wallace said, sounding weary. "At least he'll keep the property for ranching. Maybe he can even hire you to help run it."

Work as a hired hand on his own ranch? Nausea cramped Rafe's stomach. They had reached an impasse. "Just don't do anything yet."

"A week," Wallace said. "That's all I can give you."

Rafe scowled, his heart pounding, and stalked out of the office. One week wasn't nearly long enough to solve all his problems.

SUZANNE CASHED HER CHECK at the teller's window, then turned abruptly, in a hurry to get back to Rebecca's apartment and bake the cake before she went to the Lazy M, but she suddenly slammed into a hard masculine body. Two strong hands caught and steadied her, and she glanced up to see Rafe McAllister, all six-three of him staring down at her with laser-sharp, dark eyes.

"I'm sorry."

"No, I should have been watching where I was going," she said, shaken by the intense look of anger in his eyes. Anger and some other emotion, something much more disturbing. He was really upset about something. Had he found out who she was working for?

Then Slim Wallace stepped out of his office with a folder clenched in his hand, looking equally troubled, the mutinous stares that rippled between the two men explaining everything. They had just had some kind of meeting that hadn't gone very well. She'd dealt with enough men in the aftermath of a deal turned sour that she recognized the signs.

Rafe still had his hands wrapped around her arms, his expression stony. "Are you okay?"

She nodded dumbly, slowly extracting herself. "I guess we were both in a hurry."

A clipped nod was his only response.

Had Wallace warned Rafe he was going to lose his ranch?

A man's land is his pride. Without that, he has nothing. Rafe's words echoed in her head, followed by his mother's.

That tree is where Frank and I got married. And those tulips remind me of my mother. She loved tulips.

Sympathy welled up inside Suzanne. She didn't

know the name of her own mother's favorite flower.
Or where she and her father had married. Rafe had
all those memories of his land. He woke up and
looked out at the mountains where his ancestors had
lived and breathed and worked for generations. How
would he feel if his home was suddenly taken from
him?

She couldn't imagine, because she hadn't lived in
the same house her entire life, the way he had.
She woke up to an empty apartment overlooking a
crowded parking lot where people fought for parking
spaces like rabid beasts. Her place was only miles
away from her father's, but they rarely saw each
other. When they did, business usually brought them
together.

"I need to get going," he said in a gruff voice.

"So do I." She raised her chin a notch, uncomfortable with her own emotions.

He started past her, and her temper surfaced at his
dismissal. "What time do I need to come by the
ranch today?"

He turned around and glared at her, so hard that
her insides quivered.

"Or have you changed your mind?"

She saw the indecision in his eyes. Rafe didn't
want to want her to come, yet he did. And he still
thought he'd sway her to his side.

"Five o'clock. I've got a ton of stuff to do first."

"Five is fine. I have work to do, too." Like learn
how to bake a cake.

"Good, I'll see you then."

"All right."

"Oh, and, Suzanne, you might want to wear some regular boots this time."

Irritation crawled through her. He was actually criticizing her clothes. No one had ever said Suzanne Hartwell didn't know how to dress. "Don't worry, cowboy. You won't be disappointed in what I plan to wear."

His eyes shot up, and she realized how suggestive her comment had sounded. But the sudden spark of desire in his eyes that replaced the troubled look was so much nicer she didn't care; she'd have to pick out something that would rattle him even more.

After all, it wasn't fair for her to be the only one wrestling with this crazy desire.

RAFE PARKED IN FRONT of the Hotspot, still contemplating Suzanne's parting remark. What did the woman plan to wear to his ranch? Something soft and seductive?

To ride in? Not likely.

Still, he indulged his imagination, conjuring images of her dark exotic hair spread across bare shoulders, a low top veeing down to reveal enough cleavage to tempt a man to want to see more, and jeans that rode low enough on her hips to let him glimpse her bare flat belly.

Scrubbing his hand through his hair, he fought the images, reminding himself she was off-limits. A definite danger to his lonely libido.

And a distraction from problems that seemed almost insurmountable.

Shaking off the images of Suzanne, he slammed the truck door and strode into the bookstore to pick up his mother. She was standing at the register talking to Rebecca Hartwell Emerson.

"Thanks for stopping in, Mrs. McAllister," Rebecca said. "I hope you enjoy those books."

"Oh, I will, dear," Rafe's mother said. "And thanks for the chat. It's lovely to see you again. Marriage certainly agrees with you."

Rebecca blushed. "I'm enjoying it."

"I keep telling Rafe that he needs to find himself a bride. Don't you think so?"

"Mother," Rafe cut in, "Shouldn't we be going?"

"He's so ornery these days." She offered Rebecca a knowing smile as if the entire female population had some secret he didn't know about, as if all the Hartwell women had decided to conspire against him. "A good woman would change his disposition all right."

Rebecca simply smiled at him, and he tipped his Stetson in a polite gesture, then ushered his mother toward the door, wishing for once she could move that walker a little bit faster. He wasn't normally a man to blush, but all this matchmaking talk was downright embarrassing.

"What time is Suzanne coming over?" his mother asked when they'd settled into the car.

"Five o'clock. I told her to wait until I got some work done first." He heaved a sigh and hit the gas.

"I don't have time to baby-sit her all day. I've got much more important things to do. Like run the ranch."

"Then maybe you should get Bud to give her riding lessons."

He clenched the steering wheel tighter. "No, that's all right. I...the insurance might not cover him."

His mother pursed her lips as if fighting a smile and turned to stare out the window. But the twinkle in her eye suggested her matchmaking plan wasn't over.

Maybe he should relay Suzanne's opinion about the new development, that if it was up to her, the ranch he and his mother loved would be replaced by a damn mall.

He took another look at the syrupy smile on her face, and, remembering how pale she'd looked before, opted to remain silent. His mother liked Suzanne, and he couldn't stand to disappoint her.

He'd have to deal with Suzanne Hartwell himself.

Chapter Nine

Something was burning.

Suzanne raced into the kitchen, waving her hands around as she fought through the smoke. She threw the oven door open, and thick black smoke swirled out like a funnel cloud. The smoke alarm suddenly shrilled, and she reached for the cake. Yikes! She burned her fingers.

"Jiminy Cricket." Shaking her stinging fingers, she turned and grabbed potholders, then removed the steaming cake pan. A black blobby mess oozed over the edge of the pan, and the center had sunk, forming a muddy pit.

What had gone wrong *this* time?

It was the third time she'd tried to bake the cake and failed. She'd thought the third time was supposed to be the charm.

Wincing at the still-screeching smoke alarm, she shoved the pan on top of the oven, opened the kitchen door and tried to wave the cloud of smoke outside. The alarm continued to buzz. Her ears ringing, she grabbed the broom and beat the infuriating thing into silence.

Good heavens, what a nightmare. Exhausted, she sat down and blew her hair from her eyes. She was a culinary disaster. A complete failure.

How could baking one little cake be so darned hard?

The clock on the wall chimed, reminding her she was going to be late for her riding lesson, so she tossed the cake into the trash, dumped the pan in, too, knowing she'd never be able to clean it, then ran to the bedroom to finish dressing.

Earlier, she'd teased Rafe about wearing something he would like, so she pulled on her black lace bikini underwear and matching bra, then dressed in jeans and a black cotton shirt, leaving the top two buttons open to reveal just enough skin to tease him.

But what about the cake?

Oh, well, she would just stop by Mimi's coffee shop and pick up one. If she brought a silver tray from Rebecca's cupboard and sliced the cake, then placed some garnish in a few strategic places on the platter, no one would ever know she hadn't baked it herself.

After all, she *had* baked a cake, three cakes to be exact. Did it really matter if the one she took to Rafe's wasn't one of those monstrosities?

RAFE WORKED ALL AFTERNOON breaking the new quarter horse. Progress was slow, but he'd finally coached the coppery-brown horse into dropping his defenses, and had managed to rope him and lead him around the ring a few times. His chest swelled with the pride of accomplishment as he unhooked the rope. He didn't want to push too hard today. Salamander had already conceded to the first steps in his training. Rafe would lose ground if he pushed him beyond his limits too quickly. He had to gain his trust, a task that took time. And patience. Both of which he had in spades when it came to horses.

Women were a different matter.

His patience with seeing Suzanne Hartwell and not touching her had worn thin. He was almost starting to like the woman. A far more dangerous situation.

Palo Romerez pulled his truck and double horse trailer up the drive and parked just as Rafe emerged from the barn. The young man looked sheepish as he approached.

"Come to check on Salamander?"

Romerez dug his booted heels into the dirt. "Actually, I came to tell you I have to move them."

"What?" Rafe squinted in the afternoon sun. He'd hoped to get more boarders, not lose the ones he had.

"I'm sorry, Rafe, but I've found another trainer."

Rafe frowned. He'd known Romerez for years, had always valued his friendship. And, although the man sometimes ran short on money, they had exchanged services before. Palo helped him during spring roundup and Rafe worked with his cutting horses. Of course, Rafe still had to charge him for boarding, but his reputation as a trainer was growing. Or so he'd thought. One reason he didn't understand why he hadn't received calls for any new boarders.

"What's really going on, Palo?"

"I got an offer for steady work over at the Four Stars, and free boarding comes with the job. Plus I get to learn from their trainer."

Landon. Rafe should have known the man would do whatever he could to make things more difficult for Rafe. Next thing he would be stealing Bud and Red away from him.

Losing Palo's boarding fees would hurt. That money had helped pay Bud and Red's salaries.

"I'm really sorry, Rafe, but I have to look out for my family." Palo's ruddy features looked weathered. "Geraldine's pregnant, you know."

"No, I didn't. Congratulations." Rafe wanted to put his fist through something, but he understood Palo's problem. One reason he didn't need a wife or family himself. He had nothing to offer them. He certainly couldn't fault Palo for taking care of his own.

"You need help loading him up?" Rafe asked.

Palo looked past Rafe at the corral where Salamander pranced. "No, thanks, man, I can get him. I'll be back for the others later on."

Frustrated, Rafe watched Palo load the quarter horse, his hands knotted around the fence. Then he turned and saw Suzanne Hartwell in the front yard and frowned. Did she have any idea that his life was falling apart around him?

SOMETHING WAS WRONG with Rafe. Suzanne had an insane urge to go to him and tell him that everything would be all right.

Yet, how could she do that when she herself was supposed to be taking advantage of his problems?

"You are so sweet to help me with my garden," Mrs. McAllister said. "I just couldn't reach those weeds to pull them."

"It's no problem," Suzanne said. "I'm not much of a gardener, but I enjoyed hearing all about your flowers." At least she hadn't lied about her gardening ability. But she couldn't have faked her lack of knowledge. The first time Rafe's mother had mentioned pruning, Suzanne had known she was lost.

"Your mother wasn't into gardening?" Mrs. McAllister asked.

"She died when I was little," Suzanne said, dumping the weeds into the wheelbarrow. "I have no idea if she enjoyed working in the yard."

"Oh, I'm so sorry, hon." Mrs. McAllister touched the brim of her straw sunhat. "That must have been very difficult for you."

Suzanne shrugged. "I imagine it was hardest for my dad, raising two daughters alone."

"Yes, but young girls need their mothers around, too. You must have missed her terribly."

"Can a person really miss something they've never had?"

Mrs. McAllister removed her gardening gloves,

her expression so tender it moved something inside Suzanne's chest. "I think you already know the answer to that question, dear."

A surge of sadness enveloped Suzanne. Why did this woman make her think about things she had never let bother her before? Why did her companionship spark such a desperate need to have known her own mother? To belong to a family.

She *had* a family—her father and Rebecca. Yet both of them were newlyweds now. Both had a special person in their lives—someone who loved them. And although her father had been married several times, she sensed that Eleanor might really care for him. That this time he might have more than a trophy wife.

"Are you all right, dear?" Mrs. McAllister asked.

Suzanne opened her mouth to reply, but her breath caught when Rafe suddenly appeared, glaring down at her. She'd watched him working with the horse when she'd first arrived. She'd been mesmerized by his quiet manner, by the strength in his slow movements and the agility with which he'd coached the animal into trusting him. His whispers to the animal had spurred a longing deep inside her.

What would it feel like if he whispered to her in that gruff voice? She'd probably eat out of his hand, as well.

RAFE DID NOT WANT TO KNOW why his mother had asked Suzanne if she was okay or why, for just a moment, he'd seen a look of longing in Suzanne's eyes.

What would Suzanne Hartwell have to be sad about?

"Rafe, Suzanne helped me with my gardening while you were busy."

"Really?" The woman kept surprising him. Somehow she didn't seem the gardening type.

"I simply pulled a few weeds," Suzanne said. "It was no big deal."

Mrs. McAllister blushed. "It is to an old lady whose knees won't allow her to bend down anymore."

"You're a regular do-gooder, aren't you?" Rafe said, knowing he sounded surly. But his day had been crappy and the thought of spending time with Suzanne tonight, especially riding at sunset, was giving him a case of the wants.

He wanted to touch her and kiss her and forget his problems for a while. He wanted to make that sad look on her face disappear.

"You look worn-out, son. Let's have a bite of dinner before you two go riding."

"Suzanne probably has other plans."

"Actually, I don't." She tucked a strand of that dark hair behind her ear, a turquoise earring glistening in the fading sun. "But if you don't have time tonight…"

He took one look at his mother's hopeful face and couldn't refuse.

He told himself his reluctance to entertain Suzanne had nothing to do with the fact that seeing her had brightened his miserable day.

IN SPITE OF THE TENSION simmering between her and
Rafe, and the fact that he had glowered at her from
across the table, and that after his shower he smelled
enticingly of soap and shampoo, Rafe's mother made
Suzanne feel so welcome, she totally relaxed. "This
is delicious, Mrs. McAllister," Suzanne said. She
had never eaten chicken and dumplings and homemade cornbread and thought them tasty.

"Thanks, I let Maria have the afternoon off so I
could have the kitchen to myself."

"Mother, she's supposed to be taking over the
chores so you can rest."

"Nonsense," his mother said. "I felt fine today.
A body will go plumb crazy lying around doing nothing all the time." She glanced at Suzanne and
winked, and Suzanne realized that Rafe's mother was
trying, very coyly, to set her up with her son.

Guilt swamped her.

Why hadn't she recognized Mrs. McAllister's intentions before? Because she'd been so busy with her
own agenda, concentrating on avoiding falling for
Rafe's macho cowboy image and thinking about how
to convince him to sell his land to Horton Developers.

But what if he didn't sell? Had James really explored the alternatives? Would Rafe lose his ranch,
anyway? Would she actually be doing him and his
mother a favor by offering them enough money to
buy a smaller place they could manage, maybe put
some money away for retirement or a vacation for
Mrs. McAllister?

"How was your day, son?" Mrs. McAllister asked.

"Fine." Rafe offered no more, and Suzanne wondered why his reply sounded so clipped.

"What was that horse trailer doing out there? Did you take in some more boarders?"

"No." Rafe washed his dinner down with a hefty swallow of tea. "Palo Romerez pulled his horses. He's taking him to Landon's." Rafe stabbed a piece of cornbread and slathered butter on it. Suzanne couldn't imagine a man with a healthier appetite. Did he approach lovemaking with as much passion?

He was so committed to his mother, to his ranch— if he ever fell in love with a woman, would he be as committed?

"Seems Landon offered him a sweet deal to work for him."

"You mean he bribed him, to steal him out from under you," Rafe's mother said. "That no-account cuss. He's been trying to wheedle our land away from us for years." She turned to Suzanne. "Used to hound Frank all the time to sell."

Suzanne shifted uncomfortably. So, losing the boarders was the reason Rafe had been so upset. Rafe wiped his mouth with his napkin and stood, then began gathering dishes. Mrs. McAllister pushed back her chair and reached for them. "Stop that right now, son. You've worked hard enough on the ranch today. I'll do the dishes while you take Suzanne for that ride you promised her."

"But you're not supposed—"

"I'll help Rafe with them," Suzanne said, jumping into action.

"No, dear, Maria will be back any minute. She'll help me. You serve the cake you brought and get the coffee. Then you two take your ride." She smiled wistfully. "That is, unless you want cake and coffee afterward."

"You baked a cake?" Rafe asked, his surprise irking Suzanne.

"Yes, why don't you try some."

Minutes later Suzanne stared at the raptured look on Rafe's face as he consumed the dessert. The man did eat the way he worked, with passion and unabashed masculinity. Again she wondered if he made love the same way.

He licked the last of the chocolate crumbs from his finger, and she imagined that tongue trailing over her. "I have to admit that was delicious." His dark eyes met hers, enigmatic, sexy, brooding. Filled with hunger for more. "Obviously I was wrong about you being able to cook."

She met his gaze with a challenging smile. "You might find you've been wrong about a lot of things concerning me."

He arched a brow and Suzanne realized he had accepted her challenge. She was ready for the games to begin. No more pussyfooting around the fact that she found him attractive.

And that he had missed some undeniably good qualities she had. If Rafe didn't like her, she wanted to know why. Or at least she wanted to prove him wrong and show him that he had misjudged her.

RAFE STUDIED SUZANNE as they saddled the horses and rode out to the northernmost pasture, bordering Pine Ridge. He had been wrong about Suzanne being able to cook. Had he misjudged her about other things, as well? Did she have secrets that would negate all the things he'd thought about her when they'd first met?

Was she really nothing like Cecilia?

Would she break his heart if he opened himself up to her, or would she turn out to be the sensitive, caring woman he sensed lay beneath the surface of her beautiful tough-girl facade?

They passed the stream again and his favorite clearing, then rode toward Summit Falls, the place he had called a sanctuary as a child. Orange and yellow lines painted a portrait in the sky, the purple hues of dusk cloaking the treetops with a surreal glow. The mountains rose before them, a burst of spring dotted with new buds blossoming on branches left bare from winter.

"It's beautiful," Suzanne admitted.

He was so tired of fighting this attraction to her, of being alone. With everything else going wrong in his life, didn't he deserve to have a moment of pleasure? A small amount of comfort...

He guided Thunder along the trail to the waterfall, admiring Suzanne's natural riding instincts.

The forest suddenly opened up, and the sound of

gushing water brought his head up. He pivoted to see Suzanne's reaction, and couldn't help but grin at the wide-eyed, look of awe in her beautiful eyes.

"It's breathtaking," Suzanne said.

"I know. I've been coming here all my life." He guided Thunder to the edge of the pool where the waterfall flowed over jagged rocks, and tied him to a tree, tying Blondie beside him. Then he reached up his hand and offered Suzanne a lift down. She slid her hand in his, her smooth skin sparking desire low in his belly.

"Whenever I got mad at my dad or was tired of working after a long hot day," Rafe said, "I'd come up here to clear my head."

"I can see why." Suzanne's hand felt small in his, and although he'd expected her to protest, since he hadn't exactly been welcoming earlier, she followed him along the trail. They climbed over a tree stump, then Rafe sat down and pulled off his boots.

"What are you doing?" Suzanne asked.

"Taking off my boots."

"I can see that, cowboy." She rolled her eyes, then looked toward the water, the truth dawning. "You're kidding, right? You're going in?"

"Yep." He tossed his socks over a rock.

Suzanne's hands went to her waist, drawing her shoulders back and jutting her breasts out. He had to look away to keep from staring. "Isn't the water freezing?"

"That's what makes it so invigorating." He teased

her with a lazy grin. "Why, city girl, are you too chicken to try it?"

Challenge flared in her eyes. "You'd like to think that, wouldn't you?"

He threw his head back and laughed. God, he loved her sassy spunk.

She dropped to the ground behind him and tugged off her own boots and socks. His shirt came next, then his jeans. Suzanne's surprised gasp whispered through the air.

"There's nothing worse than wet denim," he said gruffly. Ignoring her flabbergasted look at the sight of his undressed state, or maybe it was the red undershorts—he'd forgotten about that—he stood and walked into the icy stream.

It was a shock to his system as the cold water slapped his bare thighs. He told himself that the icy temperature would stem his lusting libido. But he made the mistake of turning around and saw Suzanne toss off her shirt, then skim her own jeans to reveal a matching black silk bra and bikini that completely tied him up in knots. Was this what she meant when she said he wouldn't be disappointed?

He fought the need to sweep her into his arms, to ravage her the way his primitive instincts urged him to do. Instead, he dipped his hand into the stream and splashed water toward her.

She shrieked, gave him a look that promised retribution, then scooped up a handful of water and splashed back. He laughed, dodged the spray and began to run toward the falls. Suzanne chased him,

kicking water at him. He splashed back, teasing her
to come closer to the mouth of the falls. Water cas-
caded down over the rocks, the pines and sycamores
creating a shadowed canopy above. Suzanne
laughed, shrieking again as the water grew deeper.
Not giving her time to think about it, he grabbed her,
dragging her under the falls.

She squealed and screamed as the cold water
pulsed over her head, and he laughed, shivering himself as her bare thighs and wet panties brushed his
legs. She fought for release, pushing and laughing,
and he finally looped an arm around her waist and
swam with her to the edge. Water spiked her dark
lashes as she looked up at him, her skin glistening
with the icy droplets. Her teeth chattered, so they
climbed out and he rubbed his hands up and down
her arms to warm her.

"It's the most beautiful thing I've ever seen," she
said.

"I've always thought so." Rafe's eyes raked over
her long lithe body. "That is until now."

Suzanne met his gaze with a sultry look of her
own, then laughed, one dainty hand going to her hip,
which she jutted out, teasing him even more. "Why,
Rafe McAllister, I do believe you actually paid me
a compliment. And here I thought you didn't like
me."

He couldn't help himself any longer. She was
beautiful and strong and gutsy. Her nipples beaded
in the cool air beneath that flimsy thing she called a
bra, tantalizing him, and a little shiver rippled

through her, telling him that his hungry look had aroused her. Forgetting all the reasons he shouldn't touch her, he wrapped his arm around her slender waist and lowered his mouth. ''Honey, I like a lot of things about you.'' Then he claimed her mouth, letting her know exactly how much.

Chapter Ten

Suzanne felt as if she'd been waiting forever for Rafe's kiss, as if he held some elusive key to her heart, and yet at the same time she sensed she was diving into deep, uncharted water. The emotions and depth of passion he ignited in her with his sudden hunger caused a quiver of fear to run through her.

She had never been kissed with such tenderness and heat at the same time, as if he held her reverently while knowing she had hidden desires just waiting to break through to the surface. Hidden desires she had never revealed to another man. Desires she wasn't sure she even understood, desires that only he could tap into.

When James kissed her, she had never felt that emotional upheaval in her heart. She'd thought that was a good thing. But she'd been cheating herself, protecting herself from getting hurt by connecting with someone. Was she afraid to want more? To open herself up to love? Was that what Grammy Rose had meant in the letter she'd put in her hope

chest? That she'd built walls to protect herself and
hadn't let herself fall in love?

Love? She did not love Rafe. But she couldn't
deny her attraction. He was tough and brooding, a
man in trouble, but he was also honorable, a man
who loved his land and his mother. He had scars. His
limp, plus the physical ones she'd noticed on his
back when he'd removed his shirt, all of which in-
trigued her.

Did he have emotional ones, too?

Rafe's lips touched hers, almost tentative, as he
explored her mouth with the tip of his tongue. Then
he gently thumbed a strand of hair from her forehead
and traced a path down her nose, cupped her chin in
his hand and angled his head to plunder her more
deeply.

"You taste like sugar and spice and everything
nice," he whispered.

A heady sense of need overwhelmed Suzanne. She
wanted to submit to him, to do whatever he wanted
at that moment. Just as long as he kept touching her,
murmuring sweet and tender words. As long as his
big, hard body surrounded her, enveloped her, co-
cooned her in his strength.

She dug her hands into his thick dark hair, pulling
him closer, inflamed by the rough stubble on his jaw
as his mouth trailed lower to nip at her neck. His
breath feathered the inner recesses of her ear, and
she groaned, cold water splashing her thighs as he
yanked her up against him, cradling her between his
legs. His sex pulsed against her bare midriff, and

hunger exploded between them. His hair-dusted chest grazed her bare shoulders, and Suzanne gripped his arms, excitement stirring inside when his muscles bunched beneath her fingertips. He kissed her harder, taking, seeking, claiming her as if he desperately needed her, as if he might starve without her taste.

Then his mouth fled to the soft swell of her breasts, and her legs buckled. Rafe caught her and swung her up in his arms as if she weighed nothing, his lips teasing her neck again, his breath bathing her sensitive skin. Their gazes locked, questions asked but left unanswered.

But moonlight flitted through the tall pines, sharpening the image of the sapphire engagement ring James had given her. It suddenly felt heavy, weighing down her hand.

She glanced down at her near-naked body, drenched in icy water, quivering with longing for Rafe McAllister, and guilt slammed into her.

"Rafe..."

He stared at her long and hard, his muscular arms trembling slightly as the realization of what they'd almost done sank in. His head dropped forward against hers, his voice low, filled with regret. "I'm sorry, I got carried away."

"No, it wasn't your fault." She laid her hand against his cheek. God help her, but she still wanted him. Only, he didn't know the truth about her. Good gracious, what was she going to tell James?

How could she marry him when she'd almost succumbed to another man so quickly?

And why did her body ache so much for Rafe when her mind told her he was all wrong for her?

RAFE CARRIED SUZANNE to the edge of the water and climbed out, then slowly eased her to the ground. She was shivering with cold now, her skin covered in goose bumps. He desperately wanted to warm her with his body, the old-fashioned way, but his instincts warned him to back off. Her legs tortured him, though, as they slid against his. Her smooth satiny skin was such a contrast to his own that another surge of desire rippled through him. How long had it been since he had held a woman in his arms, since he had made love to one? Since he had taken comfort in a woman's arms?

Was that all he wanted here? Comfort?

He told himself yes, even though a part of him knew the truth—that he wanted more. But he couldn't allow himself to want more. He had nothing to offer.

Her fingers brushed over the puckered skin on his back, and he tensed. Not only did he have nothing to offer, but he was a scarred man. Funny, but he hadn't even thought of the scars when he'd stripped off his shirt. Odd, since he thought he'd never forget the beating his ex-girlfriend's boyfriend had given him. Had Suzanne been repulsed?

He pulled away slowly. ''I guess we'd better get back.''

She nodded, wrapping her arms around herself as

she walked to the bank to retrieve her clothes. He wished he'd brought a towel or extra blanket but he hadn't planned this outing. Especially the kissing part.

He offered her his T-shirt instead. "Here, you can dry off with this before you put on your clothes. It's clean."

She smiled and took his shirt, patting the worst of the moisture from her arms and legs as he watched. Damn, he was envious of his own shirt.

Her gaze rose and found his, and that sultry smile returned. She saw him watching her, knew he was mesmerized by her movements, and she brushed it across her abdomen, then brought it to her breasts. He cursed, turned around and jerked on his chambray shirt, then shrugged into his jeans before he could grab her again and touch her the way he wanted.

But Suzanne Hartwell didn't deserve to be taken on the cold hard ground.

And the fact that seconds ago he would have taken her there, would have taken her anywhere he could get her, proved that he was all wrong for her.

AN AWKWARD SILENCE stretched between them as they rode back to the ranch. Finally Suzanne could stand it no longer. Nearly making love to Rafe had only increased her hunger for him, and raised more questions in her mind. Who was this man, really? "How did you get those scars on your back?"

A muscle in his jaw tightened. "It's a long story."

''I have plenty of time.''

He sent a sharp look toward her. ''Let's just call them fool's wounds.''

''What's that supposed to mean?''

''Means I got them because I was a fool.''

''I see.'' She twisted her mouth sideways. ''A woman, huh?''

''A woman who used me to make her real boyfriend jealous.''

''Ouch.'' She grew silent again. ''What about your limp?''

His laughter rumbled in the wind. ''Now, that injury came from a horse. Meanest mare I ever tried to break. Called her Hellion.''

''She threw you?''

''More than once. But this time, I hit the barbwire fence wrong.''

They'd almost reached the barn. ''Did you get back on her?''

''Of course.'' He slowed Thunder to a walk. ''I had to let her know who was boss.''

But he hadn't gotten seriously involved with another woman again, she thought. Which told her he'd never gotten over that fall.

''RAFE, COME HERE!'' Bud was jumping up and down in front of the barn, waving his hands. ''Hazel's in labor. I think she's in trouble.''

''Who's Hazel?'' Suzanne asked.

Rafe slid off Thunder and tied him to the fence.

"One of my prized breeding cows. I have to check on her."

"Can I come?"

He shrugged. He didn't have time to think about the reason for her interest. If Hazel lost this calf·or died during the calving, he'd be out a bundle. Shoving his hat more firmly on his head, he strode inside the barn and followed Bud to the back stall where the cow lay on her side, groaning and shaking.

"Get some blankets," he told Bud.

"You want me to call Doc Blackstone?"

"Yeah." It would cost him an arm and a leg, but he couldn't afford not to call the vet. He unbuttoned the sleeves to his shirt and rolled them up, grabbed a pair of rubber gloves, then knelt to check the progress. Suzanne peered over his shoulder.

"Can I do anything to help?"

"Not unless you've delivered a calf before."

She bit down on her lower lip and shook her head. He almost laughed at the look of fear in her eyes. But the situation was anything but funny. He had enough troubles without the possibility of losing one of his most prized animals.

The next hour was grueling as they watched the animal struggle to give birth. He didn't understand why Suzanne stayed, but she remained steadfast by his side, crooning soft nonsensical words to the cow. Bud had poked his head in several times, saying he'd left messages for the veterinarian but hadn't yet reached him.

Finally, sometime after midnight, Suzanne fell asleep, her head tucked on her hand as she lay stretched out on the hay next to the cow. As if the animal knew it had company, it quieted slightly, giving in to the natural pains of labor more graciously.

Rafe memorized Suzanne's features, her presence destroying his preconceived notions about her.

Finally, around three o'clock, the labor process intensified. The cow thrashed at the hay with her back legs, and Suzanne stirred, brushing her hair from her face as she soothed the animal.

"She's in pain, isn't she?" Suzanne asked softly.

His gaze met hers. "Yes, if she doesn't deliver soon and Doc doesn't get here, I'll have to help her."

Her finely shaped eyebrows rose. "Have you done it before?"

"Yeah." But it was never easy, and sometimes Mother Nature took a nasty turn.

But he didn't want to alarm her. Instead, he shrugged, wiping the perspiration from his upper lip with the back of his arm. It was hot as blazes in the barn and he was shocked Suzanne hadn't complained of the heat and animal odors. She also seemed oblivious to the dirt and hay on her jeans, the flies swarming nearby and the fact that his hands were less than clean.

Hazel grunted and roiled, thrashing her legs wildly, and Rafe grimaced.

Bud jammed his head in again. "Doc's on his way. Be here soon."

Damn. Rafe gritted his teeth as the cow's cry grew fainter. She was losing steam, he realized. Not a good sign.

Bud gave him a panicked look, and Suzanne's face twisted with anguish.

He checked her again. "She's breech," he said, trying to cover the anxiety in his own voice. "I'll have to turn the calf."

Bud grabbed hold of the cow to help hold her down in case she balked. Rafe dug deeper inside Hazel to get a good grip on the calf, then struggled for several seconds and managed to latch on to the rear. He twisted and worked, sweat beading on his forehead as he felt the calf finally moving in the correct position. The cow's breathing sounded erratic, but he finally pulled the calf. Fluids covered the animal, and it lay alarmingly still. He quickly checked it for life, the silence in the barn almost deafening.

"Is it all right?"

He held his breath, but the calf finally squirmed and moved its legs.

Suzanne and Bud cheered out loud, a car engine sounded outside, and Bud raced to greet the doctor. Rafe sat back on his haunches and prayed the mother would be all right.

SUZANNE WATCHED IN AWE as Mother Nature took its course and the cow cleaned her baby. But Rafe's worried look alarmed her. He gestured for her to follow him outside while the veterinarian examined calf and mother.

"They'll be all right, won't they?" Suzanne asked. "I mean, the mother didn't go through that agony for nothing."

"Sometimes it happens," he said, not ready to offer details. "Why don't you go on home, Suzanne. There's nothing more you can do. You look exhausted."

"So do you, Rafe. You need some sleep."

"I'll sleep when I know Hazel's all right." He rubbed his hand over his growling belly, then realized he was a mess. Oddly, Suzanne wasn't balking or running as he would have imagined.

"I want to wait and see what the doctor says," Suzanne said.

He started to argue, but Bud suddenly appeared with two cups of coffee. "Here, figured you guys could use this." He grinned at Suzanne, and she smiled, wondering what he thought about her tagging along in the barn. But he didn't comment; he simply headed back to the kitchen, probably to get himself a cup of coffee, too.

Rafe leaned back against the fence and sipped the coffee, his dark gaze unreadable as he stared up at the stars in the sky. If he lost the cow, would it cause a financial strain on him?

Sympathy swelled within Suzanne and she squeezed his arm. The simple movement brought his head down, and his dark gaze locked with hers. "What are you doing here, Suzanne?"

She closed her eyes and sighed. She had no idea, but it was the first time in a long time that she wasn't in a hurry to be someplace else. The first time in forever that someone meant more to her than her job.

And that someone was Rafe.

Thankfully, Dr. Blackstone emerged from the barn before she had to reply.

His expression was grave but hopeful. "I think she'll be fine. The next twenty-four hours will tell."

Rafe nodded. Suzanne slipped inside to get another glimpse of mother and baby while Rafe conferred with the doctor. For some odd reason, tears pricked her eyes as the calf cuddled up to its mother to nurse. A few seconds later Rafe walked in. She hurriedly blinked away the moisture, unaccustomed to such emotions.

"I guess I'd better go," Suzanne said, afraid to look Rafe in the eye.

He caught her hand, the troubled look in his eyes mirroring her own feelings. "Thanks for staying tonight."

Stunned by the gruffness of his voice, she raised on her tiptoes and kissed him. A long, slow, tender kiss that promised of things to come. Then she turned and said goodbye.

He wouldn't thank her if he knew the real reason she'd come to Sugar Hill. The truth about why she'd accepted the riding lessons.

No, he'll hate you.

All the way back to the apartment, she struggled over how to handle the situation. Should she just come clean now and tell him about her job? Should she try to convince James to look for another site for his development? He was counting on her, and she was counting on the promotion....

What should she tell James about his proposal?

Chapter Eleven

Laughter sputtered over the phone. "You helped deliver a calf?"

Anger bubbled inside Suzanne. She'd finally phoned James and he was laughing? "What's so funny about that?"

"I can't picture you on that run-down ranch in a barn with horses and cows and the smell of manure around you. You're not exactly a farm girl."

"The ranch is not that run-down, James." She closed her eyes and a beautiful landscape flashed in her mind. She saw the waterfall cascading over the rocks, the tulip bulbs beginning to sprout outside the screened porch, the magnolia tree Rafe's parents had planted when he was born, the tree where the McAllisters had married, the old farmhouse that appeared run-down but was filled with family pictures, homemade afghans and doilies and Mrs. McAllister's collection of thimbles.

The house that was a real home.

Nothing like her own condo, her father's professionally decorated estate or James's fancy place.

"James, I've been thinking that maybe we're wrong to harp on getting the McAllister land when he's so opposed to selling."

"Don't tell me you're getting soft, Suzanne. Building near Sugar Hill was your idea."

She twisted the phone cord tighter. "I just think we should look elsewhere, explore all the options. The town is in an uproar over the project—"

"Listen, Suzanne, we need a large slice of land to fulfill the plans for this development, and McAllister has the best location." He sighed, and she heard him tapping a pen on his desk.

"He's also the most vulnerable right now to sell. This deal is important to me and to our futures," James said, annoyance sharpening his voice. "And we have an investor that will be very upset if this doesn't pan out."

A silent partner?

"Maybe I can talk to this investor and explain."

"Feel free," James said quietly. "But the man behind this deal is a real stickler for business."

Suzanne winced. "Who is it, James?"

"Your father."

Suzanne literally slumped onto her bed. Her father?

So, the two workaholic men in her life had joined forces. Perhaps their business alliance was the reason her father had pushed her toward James. Or had

James proposed to her out of an allegiance to her father?

Worse now, she had to worry about her family. Her father *would* want this project brought to fruition, but once again he would be at odds with his brother, Wiley. Oh, heavens. What would the other Hartwells think when they discovered that her dad was trying to change the little town they all loved so much and that she had helped?

RAFE FINALLY DOZED for a couple of hours in the barn and woke up cold and stiff, his shoulders hunched, his lower body throbbing.

He'd been dreaming that he was standing under the icy spray of the waterfall, watching Suzanne undress. She'd been only a few feet away, her skin shimmering beneath the pale glow of the moonlight, her eyes beckoning him to come nearer. Yet, he'd reached out to touch her and the undertow of the water pulling at his feet had dragged him backward, just out of reach.

He sat up, rolled his shoulders and stretched, then scrubbed his hand over his morning beard stubble.

It didn't take a rocket scientist to analyze that dream—Suzanne Hartwell was beyond his reach.

He pressed a hand on the hay where Suzanne had fallen asleep earlier and remembered how concerned she had been over the mother cow and calf. How she'd stayed beside him all night, never complaining about the conditions but offering her silent support. She was a strong woman, a woman of substance, not the shallow rich girl he'd originally assumed her to be.

Would she be that supportive to a husband, especially one with trouble on his tail?

Husband?

What the blazes was he thinking? He did not want to get married. He certainly couldn't afford a wife, especially one with cosmopolitan tastes like Suzanne's.

His mother's matchmaking must be getting to him. That and lack of sleep. Yeah, sleep deprivation did strange things to a man's mind.

Something gold and shiny shimmered through the hay and he peered beneath the blades of straw, digging until he discovered a gold cross dangling on an expensive-looking chain. Suzanne's. He'd noticed it yesterday when she had stripped in the waterfall. Lord help him, he could still see her lithe body, water cascading over the slope of her shoulders and her breasts, her nipples beading up beneath the flimsy black lace.

His body hardened again, and he wrapped the chain around his fingers and cursed, then tried to stand. Did the necklace have some meaning for her? He'd have to ask her when he returned it.

His ankle ached and nearly buckled, and he grabbed the stall to help pull himself up. Easing his weight onto his leg, he circled the stall for a minute, giving the old ache time to dissipate. He checked Hazel one more time and sighed in relief. She seemed fine. He limped toward the house to get some breakfast before he did his morning rounds. He'd forgotten to ask Suzanne if she was coming back today, but he had a feeling she would.

As he neared the house, he found himself stopping to pick a few of his mother's flowers from her garden to put in the vase on the table. Wouldn't hurt to spruce things up a bit, add some cheer to the place for his mom and any company they might have. Maybe he'd phone Suzanne to see what time she was coming so he could make sure he'd showered before she arrived. Get his mother to use the good dishes tonight if she stayed for supper. Maybe they could even serve some of that muscadine wine.

SUZANNE WOKE WITH A START, a shiver tearing through her as if something bad was going to happen today. She instantly reached for her cross, her heart stopping when she felt only bare skin. Panicking, she sat up in bed and searched the bedcovers, the sheets, the floor, then traced her steps back to the kitchen and the den and the phone, but found nothing.

Tears burned the backs of her eyelids. She had never taken the necklace off, had worn it since the day her mother gave it to her.

No, she could not have lost it.

Nervous adrenaline kicked in, but she forced herself to retrace her steps and actions of the night before. Unfortunately, she'd been so darned tired when she'd arrived home and then so upset over the phone call with James, that she didn't remember much except falling into bed. An hour later she had scoured every inch of the apartment, the stairs and sidewalk outside and her car, but to no avail.

Her heart ached with the realization that the treasured necklace might be lost forever.

Closing her eyes, she tried to remember when she had last felt it. Had she been wearing it when she'd been in the barn that night? She'd had it on when she'd gone under the waterfall....

Images of Rafe, nearly naked, his big dark body covered in water droplets and dark hair, his muscles flexing beneath her touch, stormed back. She shook off the images, trying to focus on the necklace. Surely it hadn't slipped off in the water. If so, she'd lost it forever.

Heartsick, she phoned Rafe to see if he might have found it, but the housekeeper answered and informed her he was out working, so she left a message. She would have to talk to him later.

Forcing herself not to completely give up hope, she showered and dressed, almost tripping over the hope chest when she left the bathroom. The lacy boots and hat sat like some kind of hex from her grandmother, the simple gold band that had belonged to her twinkling in the early-morning sunlight shifting through the curtains. *Sometimes, the simple things are best,* Grammy had said.

Was she right? Had Suzanne cluttered her life with too many material things and thrown herself into her job to avoid having a personal relationship? Had she become her father?

She stopped and thumbed through the items in the

chest again. Crocheting needles—under, over, loop around, she whispered, remembering her beginner lesson with Rafe's mother. Would she someday master the skill and actually complete a project? Maybe a small blanket…a baby blanket?

Oh, mercy, was she really thinking about having a baby someday? Trying to mix career and marriage and motherhood? And what kind of mother would she be? Would she know how to raise a child, when her own youth had been virtually motherless?

And then there was the gardening book. *We planted that magnolia tree the day Rafe was born.* Would she and her husband plant a tree for their child one day? Would the child look like his father?

Shaken, she raised her right hand and studied the ring James had given her, trying desperately to imagine the two of them married, having a family, planting a tree for their baby, but she couldn't.

Stunned by the uncanny choice of items in her hope chest and their association with Rafe and his mother, she stumbled to the kitchen for breakfast. Her briefcase loomed on the kitchen table, papers spread and files stacked inside, waiting for her attention. Her life had become her job. Just like her father.

After her mother's death, he had buried himself in his work so he wouldn't have time to think about the pain, the emptiness in their house.

And he hadn't married for love since. Although she had hope for his new wife, Eleanor.

James's face flashed into her mind, along with their earlier conversation. Had he proclaimed his love to her before they'd hung up? Had he when he'd proposed? No. Did he simply want a marriage that was an extension of their business partnership?

She poured herself a cup of coffee and sat down to review the other land sites Horton Developers had originally considered. Maybe she could find a solution to this project that would satisfy everyone. Including her father. *If* that was possible.

But what about Rafe?

"MR. MCALLISTER," Maria said as soon as Rafe walked in the door. "Miss Suzanne called and asked if she had left her necklace here somewhere. Said it was a gold cross."

Rafe patted his pocket. "I found it. It must have come off in the barn."

Rafe's mother eyed him over her crocheting needles. "Do tell."

Heat climbed Rafe's neck. "Hazel was in trouble, and Suzanne stayed to see if she delivered all right."

"Uh-huh."

Rafe shook his head, knowing it would be damn near impossible to dissuade his mother from thinking like that. Especially when he was beginning to want something more personal with Suzanne himself.

The dream rose to haunt him. Suzanne was standing so close yet he couldn't touch her, the undertow kept pulling him away. It was a sign. A sign that he couldn't have her.

No, he'd best not encourage his mother's fantasies

or she'd be reserving the church and knitting baby booties.

"Mr. Wallace called from the bank, too," Maria said, handing him the message. "Said something about checking the calendar."

Rafe silently growled—Wallace's subtle reminder of the time marker on paying off his debt. "Thanks." He balled the paper in his fist and tossed it in the trash, then strode to his bedroom to take a shower. As much as he hated to, maybe he'd call Landon and drop by for a talk. Maybe there was a way he could salvage his ranch with some kind of trade-off with Landon—anything so he wouldn't lose the Lazy M. Then he could swing by Suzanne's and give her the necklace.

SUZANNE ENTERED Mimi's coffee shop, her nerves on edge. Her father had phoned only minutes earlier saying he needed to talk to her. He'd already had dinner with Rebecca and simply wanted coffee and dessert with her, his tone indicating this was a business meeting, not a family reunion.

After talking with James, she should have expected the call.

She only wished she'd discovered a solution to the mess she'd created with Rafe and James first.

Mimi waved to her from behind the counter, and she waved back. Rebecca and her father strolled in, arm in arm, and Suzanne smiled, grateful the two of them had bridged the gap that had been between them for so long. Rebecca had always been such a shy young woman that Suzanne had felt the need to protect her. But her relationship with her new husband had certainly changed all that.

"Hey, sis." Rebecca hugged her, her smile radiant.

"Hey, you look great, Bec. Still in matrimonial heaven, huh?"

Rebecca blushed. "Yes. Are you surviving in my old apartment?"

Suzanne nodded. "It's great. Thanks for letting me stay there."

"No problem. Any news on the er…situation?"

Laughter teased Rebecca's eyes. Remembering the way her sister and cousins had jumped to assumptions about Rafe and the hope chest the night they'd eaten dinner, Suzanne gave her a pleading look.

Their father cleared his throat, and Suzanne glanced his way. Perspiration dotted his forehead, and his complexion looked slightly ruddy. "Dad, are you okay?"

He nodded, rubbing wearily at his stomach. "Just tired and full. Rebecca cooked a huge dinner for me."

"Must have been wonderful." Suzanne smiled.

Her father nodded again, then gestured toward a table. "I'll get us some coffee. Why don't you grab a table?"

"All right. Are you staying, Bec?"

"No. I'm meeting with the committee to discuss the town's future. Since we're business owners in the town, Mimi invited everyone over to discuss the situation. Uncle Wiley will be here any minute.''

Oh, no. Suzanne hoped that wouldn't mean trouble.

She chewed her lip, wondering if she and her father should go elsewhere, but he sat down with a slice of cheesecake and two coffees before she could suggest they relocate. Hopefully, their meeting would be short and sweet and finished before the other one started up.

''All right, Suzanne,'' her father said. ''Now tell me what's going on with this McAllister man. James phoned, and he's worried you're losing your edge.''

AS SOON AS RAFE NEARED Landon's place, he spotted Palo Romerez out by the front gate, painting it. He slowed the truck to a stop and rolled down the window. ''How's it going, Romerez?''

His friend ducked his head. ''Fine. I'm surprised you're here.''

''Guess you know Landon and I aren't the best of friends. I hope he's treating you right.''

A vein in the man's forehead throbbed. ''I heard a bunch of people were meeting at the Hotspot to talk about the land developer who planned to build that big mall.''

Rafe's hands tightened around the steering wheel. ''Tonight?''

''Yeah. About seven o'clock. Think they might be planning some sort of protest.''

Rafe chewed the inside of his cheek. Maybe his

chat with Landon could wait. If the residents kept the developer from sinking his claws into their town, then his land wouldn't be in such demand, and Wallace might cut him some slack on his debts. After all, since the developer wanted Rafe's property, Landon thought he would benefit from the deal.

Maybe Rafe would also pass word around that he could take on boarders and give riding lessons. He still didn't understand why no one had responded to his ad.

"Thanks for the tip, buddy. I'll see you later."

Romerez shuffled backward, paintbrush in hand, and tipped his hat. Rafe tipped his in return, then pressed the gas and headed toward town.

"I HAVEN'T LOST MY EDGE, Dad," Suzanne argued. "But I've been reevaluating the big picture."

"The big picture is that the McAllister property is the best land for our needs, the man is in financial trouble and needs to sell and we stand to lose a lot of money if we don't nail this deal right now."

Suzanne gripped her coffee cup. "You mean *you* stand to lose a lot of money." She might lose her job. Her promotion. Her independence. "Why didn't you tell me you were the silent partner backing this venture?"

Her father sighed and ran a hand over his beard, his cheeks growing red. "I didn't want you to feel pressured. You know I have a lot of investments."

"Is your involvement with Horton Developers the

reason you've encouraged me to be with James? You didn't suggest he propose to me, did you?''

Agitation lined her father's features. ''Of course not. But you and Horton make a great pair. You've repeatedly presented yourselves in business endeavors well, you're on the same track as far as goals go, and you seem like a suitable match.''

But, Dad, Suzanne wanted to say. I want more.

Suddenly a lightbulb went on in her head. She didn't want to have a loveless marriage with James. She wanted to feel the kind of passion her sister felt when she looked at Thomas. The kind her cousins had when they talked about their new husbands.

The kind her grandmother had mentioned in her letter.

She had to tell James she couldn't wear his ring any longer and continue pretending that they were a couple. She would call him tonight when she got home.

A commotion suddenly rang out in the back, and she noticed a throng of townspeople, her cousins and Uncle Wiley included, blustering around, pumping fists and exclaiming.

''Let's preserve Sugar Hill,'' her uncle Wiley roared. ''Stop Horton Developers from turning our town into another Atlanta suburb!''

''Yes!'' the crowd roared.

Mimi and Hannah and Alison edged closer to their father. Rebecca joined in, with rebellion in her eyes.

Suzanne clutched the table.

Her father thundered up from his seat. "Wait a minute, Wiley, what in the world are you up to?"

"I'm defending the town from rich thieves that want to steal our small-town life and values and bury them under concrete and high-rise buildings and stores."

"You don't know what you're talking about," Suzanne's father said, his voice gaining momentum with his conviction. "That development will boost the economy of this failing little town. It's a godsend, I tell you."

"It's the devil's work," her uncle yelled, his arms flapping in his orange polyester jacket. "But why in hell do you care?"

Suzanne's cousins grabbed her uncle to calm him, while she reached for her father.

But her dad shot up from the table and lurched toward her uncle, fists waving. "Because I own half of Horton Developers. I backed this project, because I wanted to save this little town from going bankrupt."

"You conceited old fart, we don't need your kind of saving."

"Dad," Suzanne's cousins said, holding Wiley back.

"You are the conceited one, you old goat," Suzanne's father shouted. "You with your wild ads and cheesy car lot, I'm—"

Suzanne's father never finished his words. His face

turned bright crimson as he clutched his chest. Her throat closed in horror as he gasped for air. Then he collapsed on the worn linoleum floor, pale as death and just as still.

Chapter Twelve

"Dad!" Rebecca's scream mirrored the one frozen in Suzanne's windpipe.

Suzanne dropped to the floor and began unbuttoning her father's shirt, the blood roaring in her ears. Her uncle Wiley raced over, Hannah, Mimi and Alison on his coat tails. Hannah checked his pulse, gave Suzanne and Rebecca a grave look, then began CPR. "Call an ambulance," Hannah said quietly. "And let's give him some space, folks."

The crowd backed up in a collective whisper of worry. Wiley grabbed his cell phone and jabbed at the numbers, calling for help, while her cousins tried to console her and Rebecca.

"I'm sure he's going to make it," Mimi said gently.

"He'll be all right, girls, he's tough," Alison said.

"Someone has to call Grammy," Suzanne said in a chocked whisper.

"Dad will," Mimi said. "And he'll call Eleanor and tell her to meet us at the hospital."

"Come on, Dad, breathe," Rebecca cried. Suzanne enveloped Rebecca in her arms, and they huddled together, shivering, while the group watched, murmuring words of encouragement as if their prayers could bring the man back to life.

Wiley swiped at the tears streaming from his eyes with a plaid handkerchief. "You can't die on us, you old codger. You're too tough to do that."

Suzanne prayed he was right. She heard her father's wife shriek as Wiley phoned her and relayed the message. Maybe Eleanor really did love her dad and they were going to make it. That is, if *he* did.

Fear tightened her chest, and she clutched at her sister. She shouldn't have argued with him.

"Dad has to be all right. We can't lose him, too," Rebecca cried.

Seconds later an ambulance rolled in, and two paramedics rushed into the room and took over. Hannah shouted commands and continued CPR while the paramedics slid him onto a stretcher and strapped him down. The family ran after them to the ambulance, she and Rebecca holding each other up.

"Can we go with him?" Suzanne asked as they loaded him into the back of the ambulance.

"We only have room for the doc."

"I have a pulse!" Hannah shouted.

The crowd cheered, and Suzanne finally released a breath.

"Get in my SUV. I'll drive," Wiley said in a shaky voice.

"Come on, Bec, Suzanne." Mimi ushered them toward Wiley's vehicle.

The ambulance door slammed shut, and Suzanne clenched Rebecca in a death grip. She noticed her uncle's ashen face and realized he was blaming himself.

As she did. After all, she had been arguing with her father before he'd spoken to her uncle. She had upset him.

"Suzanne, let's go." Alison gently coached her into the back seat where she and Rebecca huddled together.

"I'll call Brady," Alison said. "You want me to call Thomas, Bec?"

Rebecca nodded, a sob escaping. Suzanne pulled her into her arms and stroked her hair. "He's going to make it, Bec. Just keep telling yourself that."

"I'm calling Seth, too. I'll tell him to meet us there." Mimi glanced at Suzanne. "Do you want me to call someone for you?"

Suzanne simply stared at her, as Rafe's face flashed into her mind.

She had no right to call him. They weren't a couple. She shook her head, feeling lonelier than she had ever felt in her life.

It wasn't until she reached the hospital that she realized it had never occurred to her to call James.

RAFE WAS LATE for the town meeting, but he hoped to join the group at the Hotspot. When he arrived, he spotted an ambulance pulling away from the coffee shop, its siren wailing, lights flashing, a trail of cars racing after.

He searched the crowd of spectators on the sidewalk and saw Nellie Jones, one of his mother's friends, in the thick of things, so he rushed over to her. "What happened?"

She fanned her face with her hand. "Bert Hartwell, Rebecca's daddy, had a heart attack."

Oh, God. *Suzanne.* "Is...he all right?"

"They don't know," she screeched. "Dr. Hartwell did CPR, they're taking him to Sugar Hill General."

Sweat beaded on his forehead. "Was Suzanne Hartwell with them?"

She nodded, pressing a tissue to her eyes. "She and Rebecca and the other girls rode with Wiley."

Rafe nodded and jogged back to his truck. To hell with the meeting, he had to make sure Suzanne was all right.

SUZANNE'S HANDS TREMBLED around the tepid cup of coffee. It seemed as if all her cousins' husbands, along with Rebecca's, had arrived at the same time. Rebecca sat huddled in Thomas's arms; Seth stood by holding Maggie Rose while Mimi paced; Jake had cornered Wiley with coffee to calm him; and Eleanor, her father's new wife hadn't yet arrived. Hannah had gone into the E.R. with Suzanne's father.

Instead of calling Grammy, her uncle Wiley had phoned a friend of her grandmother's to go over and break the news and sit with her. None of them wanted the elderly matriarch of the family to fall ill herself from the shock. The clock hands barely rotated, the seconds ticking by slowly.

The realization that Suzanne had no one but her father sank in deeper with every passing minute. She tossed the coffee into the trash and pressed her fingers to her eyelids to stem the tears, determined not to fall apart. She had always been strong; she always would be. Dropping her head into her hands, she closed her eyes and said a silent prayer.

"Suzanne."

The thick, masculine voice took her by surprise. Then she glanced up and saw Rafe standing beside her, his eyes dark with concern, his lips pressed into a flat line, his hand outstretched in offering. Suzanne did the one thing she hadn't done in years. She let him take her in his arms, and she cried.

RAFE HELD SUZANNE in his arms, his heart aching at her tears. He hated to see a woman cry, and he sensed Suzanne didn't give in to tears easily. She buried her face against his chest, and he stroked her hair, crooning soft words to her as her body trembled. She felt fragile and delicate and he couldn't stand the thought of not holding her right now.

Memories of standing in this very same room waiting on word about his own father surfaced to haunt him. The chilling smell of the antiseptics, the sound of metal clinking on trays as nurses bustled back and forth with medicine and supplies, the fear of losing a loved one.

He hoped Suzanne's father made it. His own dad hadn't been so lucky.

Finally her sobs quieted and she raised her face, her tear-soaked hair plastered against her cheeks. He smiled and brushed the hair back, drying the moisture with the pad of his thumb. "How...how did you know to come?"

"I was on my way to see you when I heard about the meeting at the Hotspot. When I arrived, the ambulance was pulling away."

She nodded and glanced over his shoulder at the rest of her family who had obviously noticed his arrival, but were discreetly trying to ignore the fact that Suzanne had vaulted into his arms the second she'd seen him. "You were coming to see *me?*"

"Yes." He dug inside his pocket and brought out the cross. "I found this and thought you might want it back."

Her eyes widened, then fresh tears pooled in her eyes. "Oh, thank you," she whispered in a hoarse voice. "I'm so glad you found it." She hugged it to her chest, and he nodded.

"Why don't we take a little walk? Go get some coffee or a soda."

"I...I don't want to leave."

"The machines are just down the hall. Your sister can get you when the doctor comes out."

She hesitated, then finally nodded and hurried to tell Rebecca to find her the minute she received word about their father. Rafe followed behind her, well aware the other men in the room were eyeing him with curiosity.

Suzanne slid her hand in his as they walked down the hall. Then she stopped at the coffee machine and turned to him. "Will you fasten the cross around my neck? I thought I'd lost it forever."

Her voice broke again, and he accepted the gold chain, then slid it around her neck. She lifted her hair from her neck, and he groaned, tempted to kiss her bare neck right there in the hospital. Instead, his fingers brushed her nape as he closed the clasp. "It must be special to you."

"My mother gave it to me before she died." She slowly turned around and let her hair fall over her shoulders. "That was my last memory of her."

His throat felt thick. "I'm sorry. Her death must have been hard."

"I can't lose Dad now, too," Suzanne said in a small voice. "He and Rebecca are all I have left."

He wanted to tell her that that wasn't true, that he was there for her, that he always would be. But how could he make that promise when he had so little to offer? Would she even want to hear it?

"Tell me about him," he said instead, hoping to distract her. He funneled coins into the coffee machine and handed her a cup, then bought another one for himself.

"Dad's a workaholic," Suzanne began. "After Mom died, he threw himself into his job. He has a medical degree, and is the CEO of a new medical women's center in Atlanta."

"Sounds like a smart man."

"He is." Suzanne leaned against the dingy wall, staring into her coffee, deep in thought. "But he's been lonely for a long time. Probably the reason he's been married so many times."

"He's married now?"

She nodded. "The fourth time. I hope this one will stick. Eleanor's on her way. She had to drive from Atlanta."

"What happened the other times?"

"He married for the wrong reason," Suzanne said. "I think he wanted companionship, someone to help entertain his business associates." A sarcastic laugh escaped her. "But he couldn't bring himself to love anyone else after Mom died."

"That kind of commitment is unusual."

"Your parents had it," Suzanne said. "I've heard the way your mother talks about your father."

He sighed. If only his father had been equally committed. "She's the old-fashioned kind."

"What happened to your dad?" Suzanne asked.

Rafe frowned. "Maybe we'd better walk on back."

Suzanne lay a hand on his arm. "Tell me, Rafe."

The soft plea in her voice stole his breath. He had been trying to consider her feelings. Finally he cleared his throat. "He had a heart attack."

The color drained from her face.

"He died right here in Sugar Hill General."

THE MINUTE RAFE CONFIDED in her, Suzanne understood his hesitancy; he had been trying to protect her from the reality of what might happen. Yet, she also heard the pain in his voice and realized that being here had resurrected that anguished-filled memory. He had come anyway, though. Why?

Because he cared?

She wanted to believe so. But did she deserve his concern when she had been dishonest with him from the beginning?

Guilt mingled with worry and regret and fear that she had made a major mistake by not confiding about her job. Fear that when he found out, he would hate her, and that she would be all alone again.

Fear that she would lose Rafe, the man that she suddenly realized she had begun to love.

His gaze met hers. She saw compassion and other emotions that tore at her heart. She wanted to believe the love was there, that they could share the same kind of relationship Rebecca and Thomas had.

Was it possible?

"OH, MY WORD, where is my boy?" Grammy Rose burst into the waiting room in a flurry just as Suzanne and Rafe made their way back in.

The girls instantly surrounded her. "Dad's in with the doctors now," Rebecca explained.

"Are you all right, Grammy?" Mimi asked. "We didn't want you to come."

Grammy Rose waved off everyone's concern. "I couldn't stay away when my family needs me." She hugged Rebecca and Suzanne, then turned to Wiley. "John Pruitt drove me. I'm staying a few days."

Wiley leaned into his mother, his eyes glimmering with emotions. "We were arguing, Mom, I—"

"Hush now," Grammy Rose said. "I don't want to hear nonsense about anyone in this family blaming themselves for Bert's heart attack. These things just happen."

Wiley sniffled, and Mimi slid her arm around him. "He'll make it, Dad. We have to believe that."

"Right. And pray." Grammy gathered everyone together, holding hands as they formed a circle. Then they bowed their heads, allowing the matriarch of the family to lead them in prayer.

HANNAH SCOOTED BACK into the E.R. to check on their father, emerging several minutes later. Suzanne's breath felt trapped in the tension-filled air.

She had never felt closer to her family than at that second. The husbands formed a second circle, offering their support, while Rafe hovered behind her, silently giving her encouragement.

"Bert had a mild heart attack," Hannah explained in a calm voice. "But he's going to be all right."

A collective sigh of relief fluttered through the Hartwell gang.

"Can we see him now?" Rebecca asked.

"In a few minutes. The cardiologist is with him now." Hannah folded her arms across her bulging middle, and Jake reached up to massage her back. She directed her comments to Suzanne, Rebecca and

Eleanor. "Bert will need to adjust his diet, get more exercise and cut down on his work hours."

"I told him his work schedule was going to get to him," Eleanor said, her voice quavering.

Suzanne reached out and squeezed her arm, and Rebecca gave her a sympathetic look.

"I'm sure the cardiologist will talk to you in more detail."

"It…was the stress of our fight that did it to him, wasn't it?" Wiley said, rubbing at his chin.

Mimi hugged her father. "No, Dad, you heard Hannah, it was his diet. He was overworked."

"Don't blame yourself, Dad," Hannah said. "You and Bert have been fighting for years and it hasn't given him a heart attack."

Wiley frowned. "Well, that's all going to stop. From now on things will be different."

Suzanne exchanged skeptical looks with her sister and cousins. Somehow she doubted Wiley's good intentions would stick. Her father and uncle were way too different.

"Grammy always said boys will be boys," Mimi said. "Maybe that fighting between the two of you was your way of showing affection."

A nurse strode toward them, shaking her head. "Mr. Hartwell's awake, demanding to see his family. I can guarantee you that man won't be down for long."

Nervous laughter sputtered through the crowd.

"Sounds like Dad," Suzanne said.

"He'll be ordering everyone around soon," Rebecca added with a tight smile.

"I told him five minutes only and nobody can upset him. You can go in two at a time."

Grammy Rose gestured toward Rebecca and Suzanne and Eleanor. "Bec, you and Eleanor go first. Then Wiley and Suzanne can go in together. I'll go last."

Suzanne nodded. She and her uncle could both apologize for bringing on his attack.

Rebecca and Eleanor agreed and clasped hands, then slipped down the hall toward the ICU.

Rafe stroked Suzanne's back. "You okay, sugar?"

She nodded. "Thanks for coming, Rafe. I...I'm sorry I got so emotional." She pressed a hand to his damp shirt, embarrassed over her earlier outburst.

He tipped her chin up with his thumb and looked into her eyes. "You're allowed." A crooked smile pulled at the corner of his mouth, then he glanced toward her family. "You want me to leave so you can be with your family, or wait around and drive you home?"

She hesitated, then squeezed his hand, knowing her heart was in her eyes. "Wait. I don't want to be alone tonight."

He nodded, a flicker of understanding in his tender smile.

A FEW MINUTES LATER, Suzanne and her uncle slipped into her father's room. Suzanne prayed seeing Wiley wouldn't upset him, but she also understood the guilt weighing on Wiley's shoulders and couldn't deny him a short visit. He hung back in the corner, looking hesitant, even though his bright-orange tie glowed in the stark white of the room.

Suzanne inched closer, and her father opened his eyes. The steady drip of an IV cut through the silence, the sterile odor nauseating her. Her father looked pale and smaller somehow, his body attached to several tubes and wires.

"Don't you freak out over these damn machines now," he growled, although Suzanne heard affection in his voice. And worry.

How like her father to be concerned about her and Rebecca when he needed the attention.

Suzanne pasted on a brave smile and gathered his hand in hers. He touched her cheek.

"Suz, girl, I don't remember the last time you cried." His voice grew lower. "I'm sorry. I didn't mean to scare you."

"Well, you did," Suzanne admitted, realizing it was freeing to voice her emotions out loud. "So, don't do it again, okay?"

He cracked a weak smile. "Promise."

"You have to change a few things, too. Cut down on your hours, watch your cholesterol—"

"Eleanor already read me the riot act," he said, his mouth twitching again. "I have a feeling she'll be watching me like a hawk."

"Good, it's time you relaxed and let someone take care of you for a while."

"We may even take a second honeymoon. She's pretty special."

Suzanne squeezed his hand. "I'm glad you found her." And she had found Rafe. Could it work out for them? "Dad, I'm so sorry I upset you earlier. I—"

"Hush, now, Suzanne. Don't go treatin' me like an invalid. You've always stood up for what you believed in, so don't quit now. That's one thing I love about you."

"I love you, too, Dad."

She leaned over and hugged him, fighting tears again. Her father cleared his throat. "Now, get over here, Wiley. And don't go sayin' some fool thing like we're not going to fight anymore."

Wiley shuffled closer, fiddling with his tie. "Well, it's probably a good idea—"

"Hell's bells, why?" Bert bellowed. "What fun would that be? And what in the world would our families do for entertainment?"

Wiley quirked his head, then burst into laughter. Suzanne knew everything was going to be all right.

Everything except her own personal life. But she couldn't think about that now. She just wanted to go home with Rafe. To be with him for the night....

Chapter Thirteen

A few minutes later, Grammy Rose hobbled out from the ICU. "Praise be! That son of mine's going to be just fine."

"He will, won't he?" Rebecca said, still looking worried, although Thomas's comforting hand on the small of her back seemed to have calmed her.

"I didn't raise him or Wiley to be quitters," Grammy said. "'Sides, I told him he needed to hang around, that his grandkids were going to need him."

Everyone laughed, and Rebecca blushed, but Grammy Rose gave Suzanne a teasing look out of the corner of her eye. She wasn't suggesting she would wind up mommy material, was she? Rebecca would be a natural, but Suzanne had no maternal instincts. She barely even remembered her own mother, much less what a mother should do, how she should care for her children.

Suzanne glanced at Rafe, then remembered the tender way he'd helped care for that baby calf.

Would he be even more gentle with a real child? His own baby?

She shuddered. What in the world was she thinking? She was *not* imagining having Rafe's baby, was she?

She could see a dark-haired little girl or boy toddling after him, begging to learn how to ride. A miniature Stetson on top of his or her head, wearing little cowboy boots.

Good heavens, she had to get a grip.

Her cousins began to chatter at once about when they'd return to visit Bert, and Grammy Rose pulled her aside.

Rafe had sidled near the corner, looking out of place and uncomfortable, yet she noticed Rebecca approach him and introduce him to Thomas.

"Now, tell me, is this your young cowboy?" Grammy Rose asked.

Suzanne winced. "He's not my cowboy, Grammy. He's…just a man."

"Uh-huh." Grammy offered an admiring perusal of his body. "And a fine specimen, if you ask me."

Suzanne couldn't help but laugh. "He's all right."

"All right. Honey, that man is a stallion if I've ever seen one." Grammy winked. "Bet he could keep a girl happy all night and then some."

"I wouldn't know." Suzanne tugged at the collar of her blouse. "He's simply been giving me riding lesson, Grams. And showing me his property."

"Is that what men call it these days? Showing you their property?"

"Grammy!" Suzanne cupped her mouth over her hand to stifle a laugh.

"Well, darlin', I may be old, but I'm not dead yet."

Rafe glanced up and tipped his head toward her. Grammy Rose charged forward. "It's about time you introduced me, honey."

Suzanne tried to catch her grandmother before she cornered Rafe, but she was too late. The minute Grammy Rose fluttered a hand up to fan her face, Suzanne knew she was in trouble.

RAFE TWISTED SIDEWAYS, feeling vaguely out of place with this close-knit menagerie of a family and trying to behave as politely as possible to Rebecca and her husband. But the words *inquisition* and *interrogation* kept drifting through his mind.

He squirmed even more as the feisty-looking white-haired lady toddled toward him, waving her cane and grinning. "Hey, there, Rebecca, Thomas. I thought I'd introduce myself to Suzanne's young man."

She thought he was Suzanne's young man? What had given her that idea? Had Suzanne suggested something?

The waiting room grew quiet as Suzanne's cousins, their husbands and her uncle Wiley turned to watch. Rebecca giggled, Thomas raised a brow and Suzanne's cheeks flamed. A small smile twisted at the corners of Rafe's lips.

"Howdy, ma'am." He tipped his hat in a gentlemanly gesture and noticed Suzanne's surprise. Was she accustomed to rude city men? Wealthy or not, his mama had taught him manners, especially when it came to elderly women. He cradled her grandmother's hand and kissed it, liking her immediately. "My name is Rafe McAllister," he said. "You have to be one of the beautiful Hartwell women. They all take after you."

Grammy Rose hooted, then turned to Suzanne and winked again. "Why, thank you, Mr. McAllister. It's a pleasure to meet you." She hooked her arm in his, and he sensed he had an ally. "Now, tell me, don't you think our little Suzanne is just the sweetest thing since sugar on a biscuit?"

SUGAR ON A BISCUIT?

How could her grandmother have embarrassed her like that? And Rafe had played right along.

Darn the sexy man.

Besides, Suzanne was not sweet. She was sassy and independent and a high-maintenance career woman, not at all like her sweet, wonderful sister.

Her cousins hugged and said goodbye, Wiley and his new wife left with them, Grammy Rose in tow, then Rebecca and Thomas followed, but not before Rebecca offered Suzanne a little advice.

"Go for it," she whispered right before she'd cuddled up to Thomas. "And forget the land deal, sis. He's too hunky to pass up."

Hunky? Had Rebecca actually said hunky, as if they were teenagers?

Suzanne smiled to herself in the dark as Rafe drove her back to Rebecca's apartment. For a minute she'd thought Rafe was going to recant his offer and encourage her to ride with her family, so she'd had to speak up. Talk about being obvious. Maybe she was too obvious.

The minute she stepped inside, she caught her reflection in the oval mirror over the antique table in the foyer. Although darkness cloaked the room, moonlight flickered off the mirror, showcasing her puffy red eyes and disheveled appearance. Her shoulders were knotted, and it felt like days since she'd showered. But for the first time since she could remember, she didn't care that she looked rough around the edges or that she'd cried in front of this man or that she wasn't impeccably dressed. Or that she was being almost forward in stating her desire for him.

Suzanne had always gone after what she'd wanted, and she wasn't about to change for anyone.

Right now, she wanted this man.

"You look exhausted," Rafe said quietly. He flicked the light switch on the wall, bathing the room in bright light.

Suzanne flipped off the light, then stopped so his body brushed hers. The whisper of his hungry breath turned her inside out. Then he reached out and massaged her shoulders. The minute his firm hands gripped her, heat shot through her. But it was the tenderness in his touch that sent a surge of longing to her soul.

Suzanne slowly turned to him. She was offering him her heart on a platter, but she didn't care. "Rafe, thank you for tonight. For..." She caught his Stetson by the brim, then slid it off. Good heavens, he had sexy brooding eyes. And slashes of granite for cheekbones. "For staying with me."

He tucked an errant strand of hair behind her ear. "No problem. I'm glad your dad's going to be okay."

Suzanne nestled up against his broad chest, the terror she'd felt earlier resurfacing. "I don't think I've ever been so scared in all my life." It felt so good to admit her feelings for a change. Maybe Grammy had been right. It was high time she tore those walls down. Rafe was worth tearing them down for.

Rafe threaded his fingers into her hair and stroked her neck, massaging away the tension. "I know, but it's going to be all right now."

Suzanne rubbed a hand over his back, her heart thumping wildly at the way his muscles bunched. He was referring to her father's health, but she wanted to believe that everything else would be all right. That somehow they'd work out the land deal and Rafe would be able to keep the ranch he loved, the home his mother treasured. Just like her grandmother treasured her home on Pine Mountain.

Why hadn't she seen it that way before?

But she didn't want to think about land deals or her grandmother or his mother tonight. Or her lies.

She simply wanted to feel Rafe against her. Holding her. Loving her all through the night.

So she reached up and kissed him, then led him to the bedroom.

RAFE TRIED TO REMIND HIMSELF that this was Suzanne Hartwell, a fancy girl from the city, that she was temporarily visiting her family and staying at her sister's apartment, that she would be leaving and soon be out of his life. And that she might just take his heart with her. But as her grandmother said, she was the sweetest thing since sugar on a biscuit.

And it had been a damn long time since he'd partaken of either.

He was determined to savor every delicious bite.

Still, he hesitated and tipped Suzanne's chin up to search her eyes. Did she really want him, the run-down cowboy, in her bed? In her *life?*

Because as much as he wanted to steer clear of her, he wasn't sure he could settle for one night.

"Suzanne, are you sure?"

His voice sounded husky to his own ears, riddled with the echo of doubt. Damn, he didn't want to sound as if he was begging.

But seconds later his worries disintegrated when Suzanne stood on tiptoe and pressed her lips to his. He tasted the fire of her desire and caught the devilish gleam in her sensual eyes and knew that tonight he was going to make her his.

A sense of power yet soul-wrenching tenderness overcame him.

Threading his fingers through the long tresses of her silky hair, he claimed her mouth with his, seeking, searching, yearning. Her passion rose to meet his, driven from the depths of his soul. He slid his hand to her nape, caressing and stroking the sensitive skin just before he dragged his mouth down to lave her. He nibbled and suckled, his hands gently teasing her shoulders, the slope of her back, then skimmed up her body to trace a journey along her collarbone. Her sharp intake of air told him she liked his touch, the womanly fragrance of lust emanating from her almost intoxicating.

Then she went wild, stroking and kneading the muscles in his arms, his back, cupping his face to suck at his lips, trailing her own damp tongue along his jawbone and into his ear until he shuddered with hunger.

"I've never wanted a man like I want you, Rafe," she whispered into his neck as her hands teased his shirt open. Snaps popped, fingers tangled into the dark curls on his chest. He exhaled on a choked groan, then found himself standing still at the admiration in her eyes.

"You are something to see," she said in such an erotic voice his sex literally surged against his jeans. She must have sensed it because her gaze shot south, then she licked her lips.

Damn. "Suzanne."

A smile curved her mouth as her gaze met his. "I want you, Rafe. I don't care how slow or fast, but I want you."

The woman was killing him.

"Honey, I want you, too. But I want to make it good for you."

She lowered her hand and cupped him, causing fire to shoot through his loins. "I don't think that's going to be a problem."

Then she shocked him by raising her hands and twisting the buttons of her shirt. He reached out to help her, their hands becoming a frenzy of hurried movements until she tossed the shirt to the floor. Her small beautiful breasts clad in black lace taunted him, the rigid peaks of her nipples straining against fabric that was meant only to tease the imagination. Soft skin dappled in moonlight glowed like silk, begging for his kisses.

A sudden feeling of reverence filled him, and he gently stroked the ends of her hair, spreading it across her bare shoulders. "You are so beautiful." Emitting a low groan, he lowered his head and kissed her again, hard, telling her exactly what he wanted to do to her with his tongue before he nuzzled her breasts with his hands. Moaning with desire, he licked his way down to her cleavage and suckled her through the lace. Suzanne groaned with such abandonment that he felt himself coming apart. But not yet...

IF EVER A PERSON was going to die from want, Suzanne was on the hit list. She practically sobbed for Rafe to take her to heaven, but he seemed to revel in torturing her. First with his massive sexy body, now with his hands and tongue. He made a savage foray down her throat and breasts, sucking her until she thought she would explode from need. She fell into his arms, her breathing ragged as he walked her back towards the bed and they collapsed on top of the covers, all without his mouth ever leaving her. She writhed and groaned and struggled to trap his body close to her with her legs, winding them around him until she felt the hard presence of his arousal. Shifting upward, she accommodated him, the image of him naked becoming an unbearable mystery as his jeans scraped against her own.

Then he was taking them off. Hers. His. Rubbing his bare hairy legs against her smooth ones, his fingers cradling her hips and lifting her to slide off the black lace panties that were slick with heat he had ignited. Suzanne threw her head back and groaned, then perused his body with her eyes, taking in his magnificent size and the potency of his desire. All of which inflamed her even more.

"Come here, Rafe." She beckoned him to join her, but he shook his head.

"Not yet, baby."

Her breath caught in her chest as he slid on a condom and lowered his mouth to taste the heart of her. One touch of his tongue sent her to heaven. The rest made stars explode into the sky.

She screamed his name on a shudder, erotic sensations rippling through her, and begged him once again to join her. Finally she felt relief as his sex surged into her, taking her home and marking her with his personal stamp. And as he whispered her name and kissed her hair, she fell apart in his arms, clutching at him until she was sure she had clawed his skin raw.

Just as he had exposed the raw and primal part within her.

RAFE NUZZLED Suzanne's neck, pulling her naked body into his. His own body still shuddered with the aftermath of their passion, while his mind had become a muddled mess.

One time definitely wasn't enough.

He wasn't sure it would ever be enough.

"Your grandma was wrong, you're not sweet like sugar," he whispered. She jerked her head back and searched his eyes.

"You're more like molasses. Rich—" he kissed her lips, then her neck "—and spicy sweet—" he licked her neck "—and addicting."

Suzanne laughed. "And you're like chocolate," she said, trading lick for lick. "One bite makes me crave more."

They made love again, this time tenderly and slow. As they nestled into each other's arms and sleep claimed them, Rafe tightened his arms around Suzanne. Somehow he had to make things work with this woman.

He had no idea how, but he had to have her again. And again. And again.

And he did, during the night. Another time, long and slow and tender and sweet. Then another in the shower as they bathed each other. And then in the early hours of the morning, just before dawn broke the sky and the sun rose to tell them it was morning.

But the phone rang, destroying their solitude.

Suzanne curled against him, her eyelashes fluttering against cheeks pale from lack of sleep. Guilt threatened to surface, but he remembered how wild she had been in his arms and squashed it.

What if the phone call was the hospital?

He nudged her slightly, kissing her neck and blowing more kisses along her ear to wake her. The phone trilled twice more, and he finished off by blowing on her navel. She giggled and squirmed up, pushing hair from her eyes. But she was too late. The answering machine clicked on.

A man's voice spoke. "Suzanne, this is James. I tried calling last night, and wondered if you'd gotten my message. You won't believe this, but I just talked to the banker in Sugar Hill and he's ready to foreclose on the McAllister property this week."

Suzanne reached for the phone, her eyes panicked, but he grabbed her arm, their gazes locking while the man continued.

"Everything else is set. We're getting pressure to close this deal before that little town goes crazy and has time to stage some moronic protest, so I say we move today. Call me and let me know if you've made any progress with McAllister."

She tried to pull away, to stop the machine, but he shook his head.

Excitement built in the other man's voice while dread and anguish throbbed in Rafe's chest.

"Hell, it doesn't matter. We've played our cards right on this one, baby. Now it's time to swoop in for the kill."

They had played their cards right. Time to swoop in for the kill like the vultures they were.

Rafe released Suzanne's arm, his throat burning with emotions. The stricken look on her face confirmed that his speculations were true.

She was working for Horton Developers, the company that wanted to buy his land out from under him. Worse, she had been sent there to get it.

He glanced at their sweat-soaked naked bodies, and bile rose in his throat. Obviously, she'd been instructed to do anything she had to do in order to convince him to sell.

Chapter Fourteen

Suzanne froze in horror as James said goodbye and the message machine clicked off.

So did her heart.

Raw pain riddled Rafe's face. Suzanne had made the biggest mistake of her life by not telling him the truth from the beginning.

"Rafe, please—"

"Please what?" Anger hardened the husky voice that had only moments earlier murmured to her that she was molasses, the voice that had brought her to ecstasy by calling her name in the throes of his own release. "Please let you make a bigger fool out of me by sticking around."

He got out of bed, jerked up his clothes and shoved his feet into his jeans, not bothering to button them as he yanked on his shirt and grabbed his boots.

Suzanne pulled the sheet off the bed, wrapped it around her and ran after him. "No, Rafe, it wasn't like that. Please wait and let me explain."

He spun around, fury tightening those high cheekbones, the rage in his eyes darkened by hurt. "You don't have to explain. Your buddy made it pretty clear what you're doing here." His gaze flickered over her with undisguised disgust. She felt even more naked and exposed, as though he was literally stripping away the skin to smirk at the bare ugliness below.

"And it's obvious you did everything in your power to lure me to your way of thinking. What was I? Another one of your charity cases?"

"Rafe, I never..." Her voice broke, laden with hurt at his crude insult. She cleared her throat, desperately searching for some way to make things right as he pulled on his boots. "Did I mention the land while we were in bed? Or while you were kissing me?"

His angry gaze shot back to her. "No, you didn't." He strode toward her, shoving his face so close she could see the vein jumping in his jaw.

She could also smell her lingering scent on his skin.

"Just when did you plan to drop that little bombshell into the conversation, Suzanne? In the middle of a bath together? Or were you going to wait until the next time when I was inside you? Or maybe you planned to wait until the town meeting?"

Her chin quivered, the need to touch him so strong she pried one hand loose from the sheet and reached out. But he jumped back, as if appalled by her.

"The game's over," he barked. "So you can tell your friend—"

"He's my boss." Lord, she didn't have the heart
to tell him James had actually proposed to her. That
had been a lifetime ago. Before she'd come to Sugar
Hill and met Rafe and his mother. Before she'd
learned to care for him and love his land.

And before she'd fallen in love with him....

A pain crushed her windpipe as the magnitude of
the situation hit her. He would never trust her again.
And he would never believe that she had planned to
refuse James's proposal and look for an alternate
piece of land for Horton Developers, only things had
gone crazy tonight when her father had his heart attack—

"Tell your boss that my property is not for sale.
Not now." Rafe hesitated, one hand on the door-
jamb. "Not ever. Especially to you and Horton Developers."

His boots clicked harshly on the floor as he stalked
out the door. Suzanne crumpled, certain he would
never be back.

It was her fault that she had lost him.

RAFE SPENT THE BETTER PART of the next day doing
as much hard labor as he could around the ranch.
Anything to work off the anger from the night before.

Why hadn't he realized what Suzanne was up to?
Why hadn't he followed all his instincts in the beginning and stayed clear of her?

Because she suckered you in with those brown
eyes and that lush body. And then she had to go and

be nice to your mother, as if she was really a decent girl.

Because you are a damn fool when it comes to women.

He pounded the last hammer into the wooden post, wiped sweat from his forehead and stepped back to survey the corral. At least he'd put his energy into something productive today.

Maybe he'd go out and check the herd.

"You driving like a demon today," Bud said. "What's got into you, boy?"

"Nothing, just trying to get this place back in shape," Rafe said, gathering his tools.

"Stop in and see your mama a minute. She's been wanting to talk to you all day."

A moment of worry attacked him. "Is she all right?"

Bud patted his back. "Yeah, but be forewarned. She's planning some kind of dinner party and wants to rope you into it." He made a tsking sound with his teeth. "Women."

"Yeah, women."

Now, what did his mother have up her sleeve?

He walked toward the house, dread clenching his stomach as he stabbed a guess. Her sudden need to entertain most likely had something to do with Suzanne. How could he explain that his days spent with Suzanne Hartwell were over? That they had both been wrong about the woman?

That she was not the friend she pretended to be, but the enemy?

SUZANNE HAD NEVER BEEN so miserable in her life. She forced herself to visit her father that morning and found him irritable and ready to leave the hospital, so Eleanor had arranged his release and they were driving back to Atlanta. Not wanting to upset him or hear an I-told-you-so, he's-all-wrong-for-you speech, she had avoided telling her father about her relationship with Rafe.

"Suzanne, wait." Rebecca caught her in the hall. "What's wrong?"

Suzanne shrugged off her concern and did what she did best—focused on business, which was what she should have done all along. "Nothing."

But Rebecca didn't buy it. She should have been a shrink. "Tell me, sis. It might help to talk."

She doubted it. Still, moved by her sister's concern, Suzanne spilled the entire story.

"Oh, my," Rebecca said in a voice filled with such pity that a fresh well of tears exploded and overflowed down Suzanne's cheeks. Once she'd opened the floodgates at the hospital, it seemed she couldn't stop them.

Horrified at herself, Suzanne hugged Rebecca good-bye, then jogged down the hallway and outside to her car. Sunshine burned her neck, but it didn't dry her tears.

Determined to regain her focus and devise a solution to all their problems, she spent the afternoon scouring the countryside, checking out property and searching for some way she might win Rafe back. If only she could figure out a way to help him keep his ranch. But he still had all that debt hanging over him. He didn't want her working against him, but he sure as heck wouldn't accept her help, either. Stubborn old cowboy.

Stubborn sexy cowboy.

Stubborn sexy cowboy that she loved.

Finally exhausted, she drove back to Rebecca's apartment, but tears blurred her vision as she let herself inside, the heavy sense of loss and failure weighing on her. What was she going to do? Any way she handled the situation, someone would be upset with her.

If she and Rafe didn't have a future, she needed to at least keep her job.

She glanced at the ring James had given her, the huge stone sitting like a boulder on her hand. Her heart sank even further in her chest. She couldn't marry James. It wouldn't be fair to either of them. After all, now she had experienced the true kind of passion and love in Rafe's arms, how could she even think about being with another man? The hope chest mocked her from the corner, the cowboy bridal hat and boots blazing like a big neon sign, reminding her of Rafe and his mother.

A knock sounded at the door and she froze, wondering if Rafe might have changed his mind and returned to hear her out.

But the memory of the condemning look on Rafe's face when he'd walked out the door flashed into her mind. No. The idea of Rafe forgiving her was a pipe dream.

The knock grew louder.

She tried to ignore it, but the door opened and Rebecca strode inside, Grammy Rose and her cousins close on her heels.

"Suzanne, honey, why aren't you answering your door?" Grammy Rose asked in a worried voice.

"We brought you comfort food—café mochas and pecan pralines," Rebecca said.

"And we brought extra brainpower," Hannah said.

"And moral support," Alison added.

"We can even give you sex tips on snaring that cowboy," Mimi chimed.

Suzanne took one look at her loving family and realized in Atlanta she had no friends. Here, in Sugar Hill, she had family, people who loved her and…and a man she loved but had lost.

Grammy Rose held out her arms and a box of tissues, and Suzanne collapsed in her embrace. "Thanks, you guys, I could use all the moral support and brainpower I can get."

"And don't forget sex tips," Mimi said with a wink. "After all, you aren't going to give up on getting that cowboy back so quickly are you?"

"Of course she's not." Grammy Rose patted her back. "She's a Hartwell girl, isn't she? We always get our man."

"HOW ABOUT WE ASK HER for dinner tomorrow night? I'll invite Bud and we'll have a foursome." Rafe's mother placed a fresh bouquet of daisies on the table. "Maria can throw together a salad and whip up some rice and gravy, and I'll fry some country-fried steak and make one of my peach cobblers. Do you think Suzanne likes country-fried steak? Or maybe you should grill the steak outside, just in case she's one of those health-conscious city girls." She laughed and fluttered a hand. Her health had improved so drastically over the past few weeks that he hated to disappoint her. "Oh, never mind, it won't hurt the girl to plump up those curves a bit, the more to love—"

"Mother, we're not having Suzanne over to dinner tomorrow night."

"Mercy. Well, of course a smart, beautiful girl like her probably has plans on such short notice. How about the night after?"

"Not then, either."

"Oh, dear, maybe you should ask her when she's free." A look of concern tightened her brow. "You'd better jump on it, son, before some other man snatches her right out from under you."

She was a smart girl all right. Smart and deceitful. "Mother, Suzanne is not coming any night."

"What?" Her animated movements halted. "I know you've been ornery today, but you didn't say something to upset her, did you? 'Cause if you did, go apologize. Take her flowers, women love flowers."

His mother thought he had upset Suzanne? Oh, that was rich.

She pursed her lips. "I wonder if she likes daisies.

Or you could take her roses. Roses are the best. I'll let you pick some from the garden—''

''Mom, I am not taking Suzanne roses!''

She pressed a hand to her chest. ''Well, you're never going to get that girl if you don't at least try to be a little romantic.''

Well, hell, just the mention of Suzanne Hartwell's name was driving him crazy. He certainly didn't intend to romance her, not after the way she'd used him.

''I'm sorry, Mom, but I'm not going to be seeing Suzanne again.'' He spun on his heels and marched toward the door. He didn't have it in him to break her heart and tell her the truth. Better she think he was a loser in the love department.

No, he'd forget Suzanne.

But he would talk to Landon and see if he could save his ranch. He'd rather rent the land to the man who had betrayed his father than let Suzanne and her company turn it into their development.

''ALL RIGHT, you want to help your cowboy save his ranch for his mama, right?'' Grammy Rose said.

''He's not my cowboy, Grammy. He hates me.''

''Psshaw. He doesn't hate you. I saw the way he looked at you at the hospital.'' She hugged Suzanne. ''You've got your cowboy, you just need a little Cupid now.''

''I doubt Cupid will help,'' Suzanne whispered miserably.

''Sure he will. You can get him back,'' Mimi said,

her smile radiating confidence. "Let me teach you how to belly dance. Seth loves it."

Hannah rolled her eyes, one hand on her pregnant belly. "I wish I could belly dance right now."

"Is that how you snared Seth?" Alison asked.

Mimi jumped up, tied her button-down shirt up to her waist to reveal her flat belly, then rotated her hips and gyrated her stomach. "It's all in these—"

"Girls," Grammy chided softly, peering over wire-rimmed spectacles. "I believe we're getting off track."

"Right," Rebecca said. "Although maybe we could all take a belly-dancing lesson later."

Mimi gave her a thumbs-up.

"Now, let's get down to the nitty-gritty," Grammy Rose said.

Rebecca spoke up. "You know I'm against the new mall development, too."

"Me, too," Mimi agreed. "I like high fashion, but I'd rather Sugar Hill get some trendy little boutiques. You know, the funky artsy kind."

"Like the ones in Little Five Points in Atlanta," Alison said.

"They have great art galleries there that showcase local artists, too," Rebecca said.

"Pine Mountain has an entire section of antique stores, and little arts and crafts shops," Grammy added. "Pearl and Wyline sell their needlepoint pillows there. And Junior displays his woodworking projects. He sold seventy-five wooden owls last year. Made enough to buy himself a new set of teeth."

The girls giggled, and Suzanne wiped at her eyes, an idea beginning to take shape in her mind, "You might just have something there."

Her cousins exchanged confused looks.

"You want Junior to sell his wooden owls down here in Sugar Hill?" Grammy asked.

Mimi clapped her hands. "And you want me to teach belly dancing?"

Suzanne laughed. "No, well, maybe." She waved her hands and gathered her cousins and sister and grandmother together. "What do you think about this concept?"

She quickly pitched her idea, her excitement gaining momentum as they offered ideas of their own. "I'm going to call a town meeting for tomorrow tonight," Suzanne said. "But first, I'll put together a written plan to show everyone how my idea can work."

"It's perfect," Hannah and Alison said.

"I might even show some of my art there," Rebecca said, emerging from her shell even more.

"See," Grammy Rose said. "I knew if the Hartwell girls put their heads together, they'd find the answers."

Suzanne nodded. They had found a solution to the land development problem, and she had an alternate site in mind for the mall, so Rafe's property wouldn't need to be bought. But neither would pay his bills.

But how would she get back in his good graces again—and make him fall in love with her?

THE NEXT DAY Rafe had choked on his pride by cutting a deal with Landon to rent part of his property to the man for grazing rights. As he left, he met Palo Romerez at the gate to Landon's ranch. "Suzanne Hartwell did what?"

"Heard she called a town meeting to discuss the new development. Guess they'll pick up where they left off the other night."

When her father had his heart attack. Man, Suzanne was even more coldhearted than he'd imagined. It had only been forty-eight hours and she was back in business mode. Bitterness filled him. Obviously she'd never left it.

And to think she had wept in his arms and acted as if her family meant everything to her. As if he meant something to her.

Instead, her job meant more to her than he did.

"Thanks for passing on the info," he said, shifting gears. "I think I'll head to town now."

Ten minutes later he parked in front of the town hall, not surprised to find a large gathering outside. Elderly women marched in a circle, waving homemade signs painted with magic markers that read Tree-killers Go Home. A few of the old-timers chanted, "Save Sugar Hill. Save Sugar Hill."

The mayor wove through the crowd, trying to calm people, urging folks to consider the big picture and passing out Reelect Orville Lewis stickers.

Wiley Hartwell roared up with a train of cars, decorated with banners and streamers. Dozens of people leaned out the windows, waving signs, honking horns, a few shouting through bullhorns, "Don't kill off the small businessman."

The prayer wagon from the church held out lit candles, the alto part of the choir humming in the background while the sopranos sang, "Save Sugar Hill from the sinners."

Rafe shuddered at the horn-blowing, then watched in disbelief as some of the people actually drew a visible line on the sidewalk, those in favor of the development taking a stance by jumping the line to congregate together, chanting "Don't hold us back. We want progress." The other half shouted and yelled back, clustering on the opposite side like soldiers ready to defend their country from foreign invasion.

A shiny convertible roared up and out climbed Suzanne Hartwell, looking like the city girl she was in a black designer suit that hugged her curves and spelled class. The crowd virtually parted like the Red Sea as she sashayed through them to the front stoop.

Rafe folded his arms and watched, unsettled by her appearance and remembering how it felt to touch and taste every inch of those delectable curves. For one brief second, when Suzanne spotted him, he thought he detected a spark of emotion in her eyes.

Something that looked like tenderness. Or real affection.

But he'd been a sucker once; he refused to let her fool him again.

So he simply stared her down, silently vowing not to let her affect him.

SUZANNE'S HEART leaped in her chest when she spotted Rafe. But the look of hatred in his eyes slammed into her like a knife piercing her chest. She nearly buckled from the pain, but forced herself to move forward. Maybe if he heard the solution she'd come up with, he'd give her another chance. Whatever the outcome, she had to talk to him first and make sure he knew she really cared for him. That everything hadn't been a lie.

She turned to the mayor. "Why don't you get everyone inside and calmed down, then we'll talk."

He nodded, puffing his chubby little body up like a rooster ready to crow, then clapped his hands and started issuing orders.

Meanwhile, she zigzagged through the crowd until she reached Rafe, then dragged him to the corner. He simply stared at her, his dark eyes like ice. "Rafe, I'm so glad you're here—"

"Why, so you can humiliate me in public?"

Her legs wobbled beneath her at the venom in his voice. She cleared her throat, willing herself not to break down. What had happened to spunky Suzanne who could close a cutthroat deal without blinking an eye? "No, Rafe, because I think you might like my idea. That is, if you can knock that chip off your shoulder long enough to listen."

Uh-oh, her temper was taking over. Trying to protect her from the pain. But Rafe didn't know that, he simply thought she was ruthless.

"Is that what you came to tell me?"

She closed her eyes, trying to regroup her

thoughts, then opened them and searched his face for any trace of emotion other than disgust. She found none. She plunged forward, trying gut-wrenching honesty for once. "I'm sorry for the way I handled things, Rafe. I really am. But I'm trying to make up for it."

His jaw tightened, emotions flickering in his eyes. It was almost as if he wanted to believe her but couldn't.

"I don't want to hurt you or your mother. You were right to show me your land and let me see how much it meant to both of you."

He continued to stare at her, and she shifted, grasping for courage in spite of the fact that his re-action offered no encouragement. "I know how I would feel if someone made my grandmother give up her beloved house on Pine Mountain."

"Then why didn't you tell me the truth about why you came to Sugar Hill from the beginning?"

Suzanne pleaded with him with her eyes. "I…I don't know. I was going to, but then Dad had that heart attack, and…things just happened too fast."

His head jerked up. "You had plenty of time be-fore then."

"I…I know and I'm sorry." She might as well go for broke and admit that she loved him. Maybe if she made a complete fool out of herself, he would forget the fact that she had made one out of him. Not that she'd meant to, but he thought she had. "I…I—"

"Suzanne!"

Suzanne halted in horror as James jogged to her

side. He curved an arm around her and kissed her cheek. "Hey, I'm glad I got here in time. I talked to your father. He told me about the meeting."

Rafe knotted his hands into fists, clenching his jaw so tightly his words sounded as if they'd been ground out between his teeth. "You must be from Horton Developers?"

Suzanne grimaced. Oh, heavens, what awful timing. "Rafe McAllister," she said, gesturing toward James. "This is James Horton. My boss."

"And her fiancé," James said at the same time.

Chapter Fifteen

Rafe squared his shoulders to keep from stumbling backward. Suzanne was going to marry this guy?

"Engaged..." he said, spying the monster sapphire ring on her right hand. Funny how she had neglected to tell him about the man who had given it to her or its significance.

"Rafe, please, let me explain—"

James extended his hand. "We'd like to sit down and discuss some business with you."

Rafe glanced at the man's gesture of friendship and snarled. If he hadn't wanted to do business with Horton before, he certainly didn't want to touch his dirty hands now. What kind of man sent his fiancée to seduce another man to further his career? He almost felt sorry for Suzanne. Why had she let this man use her like that?

"I don't do business with people like you," Rafe said, not caring how ill-mannered he sounded.

Horton dropped his hand, his nostrils flaring. "Your attitude won't save your ranch, McAllister. I know what shape you're in financially, and how you got there.''

''James—'' Suzanne clutched at his elbow, and Rafe grimaced, an irrational seed of jealousy eating at him just seeing her touch another man. He wasn't supposed to care.

Steeling himself against his foolish feelings toward her, he directed his comment to Horton, his tone lethal. ''What exactly is that supposed to mean?''

''It means I'm aware your father had a gambling problem and—''

Suzanne pulled at the man again, and Rafe exploded.

''My personal life is none of your business.'' He refused to let the man voice the ugly truth about his father's affairs in public. If someone else heard and told his mother, she would be devastated.

Did Suzanne already know? Had she been holding the information as some kind of wild card to play in case he didn't cooperate?

The mayor bobbed his head out. ''Ms. Hartwell, I believe I've got everyone settled down now. We're ready to begin.''

Suzanne twisted her hands together, looking agitated. ''Rafe, James, just come in and hear my suggestions. I have a solution that will make us all happy.''

Rafe failed to see how that was possible. Did she plan to still sleep with him and marry her rich boyfriend? ''There is nothing either one of you have to say that I want to hear.'' Rafe spun on his boots and thundered away, humiliation and hurt knotting his stomach.

WHEN RAFE HAD LEFT the night before, Suzanne had thought things couldn't get worse. But his ice-cold attitude toward her had now dropped well below the freezing point.

And she still had to deal with James.

"Are you coming, Ms. Hartwell?" Mayor Lewis brushed the three hairs on his balding head in an obvious attempt to prove he still had hair.

"Yes." Knowing Rafe needed time, and she had her work cut out for her, convincing the town to go with her idea, she headed inside. James followed.

"I'm sorry, Suzanne, I didn't realize that guy was such a jerk or I wouldn't have sent you down here alone."

Suzanne winced. "He's not really that bad. But his property means a lot to him."

"Yeah, but geesh. Think of the money he can make."

"Not everything is about money, James," Suzanne countered, suddenly realizing that his entire value system revolved around dollar signs. In fact, except for his marriage proposal, which had sounded more pragmatic than romantic, most of their conversations had been about business deals, profits and earnings and stock options.

"Here, here. Let's have some order," the mayor bellowed.

Suzanne ignored James's perplexed look, wove

through the aisle separating the two hostile groups and took the microphone. As she gazed out into the crowd, she spotted her uncle Wiley. Beside him sat Grammy Rose, her three cousins and Rebecca. Thank God her family was behind her, she thought as they each gave her a thumbs-up.

Still, her heart ached. If only Rafe had stayed and heard her idea.

Maybe then he would realize she wasn't the cold, heartless female he thought her to be.

"Ladies and gentleman," Suzanne said. "I work for Horton Developers—" a round of boos circulated the room, but Suzanne waited them out, then continued "—but please hear me out."

"Yes, hear the girl out," her uncle Wiley shouted.

The other Hartwells clapped, and Suzanne smiled her thanks. "I understand the controversy surrounding the proposal for the new mall project, and I've taken everyone's concerns into consideration. Each of you has made some valid points, but I think I've created a solution that will suit all of you as well as alleviate your anxiety."

"Let's hear it, then," the mayor said.

Suzanne displayed the flow charts and diagrams she'd worked on all morning. "Instead of the shopping mall we had originally designed, I've drawn up a scale model of a different type of cluster that would lend itself to the small-town life you all love, bring in extra revenue for the town and showcase some of your own local talent."

The crowd grew quiet, their interest captured.

"How you gonna do that?" an elderly woman asked. Suzanne smiled to reassure the woman, then noticed that Rafe's mother was sitting next to the lady. Mrs. McAllister fluttered a wave, and Suzanne nodded, wondering if Rafe had told his mother about her deception.

"Yeah, how are you going to do that?" Bud, Rafe's ranch hand shot up from his seat, and Suzanne gripped the edge of the podium, his scrutinizing look not as friendly as Rafe's mother's.

"With a development that consists of specialty shops housing clothing boutiques, an art gallery, antique stores, as well as arts and crafts stores that could sell local wares created by the citizens of Sugar Hill. In addition, we could incorporate a country restaurant and an old-fashioned drugstore that will add atmosphere and enhance the historical feel of the town."

"I could sell my pottery there instead of out of my barn," a young woman with a baby in her arms said.

"And I can put some of my sewing there," a middle-aged woman with a big straw hat said.

Rebecca's husband, Thomas, piped up. "Rebecca has some lovely paintings to sell."

"But where would we put it?" an old-timer in coveralls asked.

"There are some empty warehouses over on Dothan Street," Suzanne said. "I've already checked them out."

"You mean right downtown?" the mayor asked.

"Yes, it can be a town project," Suzanne said. "With the profits, you'll probably be able to give some of your existing businesses a facelift, too."

"The Hotspot could use a facelift," Mimi said.

"So could my law office," said Suzanne's aunt.

"And I need some renovations to my bridal boutique," Alison added.

A gray-haired lady with a bouffant hairdo waved a handkerchief. "We could set up a place to teach arts and crafts, maybe even have a quilting bee in the back room."

"I vote for that!" a woman beside her chirped. "We could even offer craft classes."

"To cut down on cost, you can share space in the warehouse and curtain off different areas to make booths," Suzanne explained. "Imagine a big flea market atmosphere."

"My husband can sell those fabulous horse head canes he makes," Dottie Berger said. "He hand carves each one himself so no two look alike."

"And I've always dabbled in antiques," another young mother said. "I could have my own booth."

"And Ruby Jean can sell her famous homemade fig preserves and jellies," a blue-haired woman with a hearing aid shouted.

Suzanne nodded at their enthusiasm, but James frowned at her from the side. "You're talking about doing this instead of the multilevel development we'd planned?"

"Yes. This project will fit the town," Suzanne said, her voice growing stronger, "increase revenue and tourism, and offer something more unique than your average everyday shopping center. Horton Developers can help these people refurbish their own town and utilize their talents, and the mall can be built farther out of town. I've already located another piece of property that will meet Horton's needs.''

The town cheered, the locals throwing out suggestions for the craft store. Suzanne beamed, grateful they had liked her proposal.

Well, everyone except James.

He was probably going to like her next announcement even less. She had to tell him that she didn't intend to marry him.

''OH, MY WORD, you should have been there, Rafe,'' Mrs. McAllister tittered. ''Suzanne Hartwell is a genius.''

You mean the deceiving, lying, engaged woman who used him, then threw him away?

Rafe bit back the comment burning the tip of his tongue. ''A genius, huh?''

''Yes. She had the entire town eating out of the palm of her hand.''

''I imagine she did.'' Just like she'd had him eating out of the palm of her hand. Hell, he'd been on his knees—

''Maria, set an extra place, will you?'' His mother said, grinning. ''We're having a guest for dinner.''

''Yes, ma'am.'' Maria hurried to the kitchen to retrieve another place setting. The smell of homemade fried chicken, mashed potatoes and peach cobbler wafted through the double doors, and Rafe caught the implication.

Oh, hell. "You didn't invite Suzanne Hartwell to dinner, did you, Mom?"

Disappointment fell across her face. "Actually, no. But not for lack of trying. She and that man from Horton Developers skipped out of there so fast I didn't get a chance to ask."

Was Suzanne off with Horton now? Was she kissing him, holding him...

His stomach rolled at the thought.

"So, who's the extra plate for?"

His mother's cheeks turned pink. "Uh, Bud's going to join us."

Right. She'd mentioned inviting him before. But why was his mother blushing?

"Yes, it's really no big deal, son, but he's been so nice to me lately. And he drove me to town today to the meeting. The poor man needs a decent meal every now and then." She patted her hair, which looked as if she'd just come from the beauty shop. And if his eyes were working properly, she'd had some kind of color put on it. The gray had completely disappeared.

"You don't mind do you, Rafe?"

Rafe shrugged. "I guess not. I like Bud." Was the man trying to woo his mother?

Not that he should care if they got together. Bud was a good guy, a hard worker, although financially he didn't think the man had much to show for himself. But he wanted his mother to be happy. And she had seemed so much happier these past couple of weeks. He'd thought it was because of Suzanne, but maybe she had a crush on his ranch hand.

After what his dad had done, she deserved to find someone else.

He glanced at the table and winced. If they were heading toward a romantic relationship, he would feel like a fifth wheel at dinner. "Mom, tell Maria not to bother to set an extra place. I'm going out tonight."

"Oh?" The curiosity in her eyes cut him to the bone. She thought he was going to see Suzanne.

He pictured Suzanne with Horton, though, and strode outside. Maybe he'd drop by the Dusty Pub and drown his sorrows with a pitcher of beer. Anything to take his mind off the fact that his mother had a new love in her life, while he had failed miserably in his own.

As SOON AS the meeting broke up, James cornered Suzanne. "I really wish you'd discussed this new plan with me before you presented it."

"You don't like the idea?" Or did he simply not like being upstaged by a woman?

James ran a hand through his hair. "No, it's a fine idea, I just wish we'd discussed it first."

"I think you'll like the other spot I've found for your mall," Suzanne said. "It's about twenty-five miles out of town, but it has great access to the expressway, and you won't have to deal with the backlash of this town's protests."

James twisted his mouth sideways. "All right, I'll look at it." He offered his first smile. "You usually do have good judgment. But I thought you were losing your edge for a minute when you first brought up the idea of this hokey arts and craft village."

"It's not hokey," Suzanne said. "There are some talented people in town, and their uniqueness will draw tourists to visit. With the mountains behind them, the possibilities are endless. I can see a bed and breakfast going in, maybe a row of antique stores. Horton might want to think about putting some rental cabins in near Turner's Point. The stream that runs through that area is great for fishing, a perfect mountain vacation."

James planted both hands on her arms and pulled her to him, then kissed her. "Thank God you're back. I thought I'd lost you to all that sentimentality, when all along you've had your head in business."

Suzanne tasted the guilt on her lips and forced herself not to visibly wipe off his mouthprint. She wanted Rafe's approval, Rafe's kiss, Rafe's hands holding her.

"James, there is some truth to what you said," she said, vying for honesty.

His eyebrows creased together. "What do you mean?"

"That I...the sentimental stuff." Oh, heck, she couldn't admit that she'd fallen for Rafe McAllister, not when he hated her. She did have some pride left, albeit not much. But she had to break it off with James.

So she simply blurted out the truth. "I can't marry you, James."

His stunned expression would have been funny if she hadn't detected a slight bit of hurt to it. Or maybe it was just his pride that had been hurt. He had never mentioned love. Not once.

And his kisses certainly didn't have the passion she'd experienced with Rafe.

"You can't marry me?" James said dumbly.

"That's right." She slid the ring off her finger and folded it into his hand. "I...I do care about you, James, and I admire your talent on the job, and I...I appreciate the offer."

"You appreciate the offer?" he asked in an incredulous voice.

"Yes, but I don't love you, James."

"Who said anything about love?" Anger hardened his voice. "We had a good thing, Suzanne. We get along, we work well together, just look at how this deal turned out."

"Yes." Suzanne's heart gave a pang. "Just look at how it turned out." Then she left him standing inside the town hall and went to nurse her broken heart.

Everything had worked out for the town, although she didn't know if she could return to Atlanta and work with James now. Not that he would want her to....

But Cupid had failed miserably. No, Cupid hadn't failed. She had.

She was the screwup, the one who had hurt Rafe.

And she would never forgive herself.

Needing a distraction, she decided to visit her father. She'd check on him and tell him in person about her proposal. Resigned, she climbed in her car and drove out of town, thoughts of Rafe flooding her as she passed the Dusty Pub, the bar where she had first met Rafe. She spotted his purple pickup truck, the one that he hated, and slowed.

He was inside now. Having a drink at the bar.

She could see him tipping that Stetson toward her the night they'd met. If she were completely honest with herself, she would admit that she'd fallen a little bit in love with him that first night when he'd held her in his arms and danced with her. And the day he'd given her riding lessons. And that day in the waterfall.

Pain seared her chest.

Was he holding another woman in his arms right now? Crooning soft words in her ear until he danced his way into her bed and her heart?

Chapter Sixteen

Rafe frowned at the juke box; Elvis's words about being lonesome tonight ringing way too close to the truth. Damn it, he was lonesome and he didn't like the feeling. Even worse, he had been at the pub for over an hour, three women had hit on him, and he had been unable to muster enough interest to even buy one of them a drink. And the last one had been a blond bombshell with blue eyes that could sink a man, and boobs that would have once sent him over the edge.

But the blond didn't compare to Suzanne's dark hair. Or eyes.

Suzanne Hartwell had ruined him for other women.

Which made it ten times more difficult to forget her.

And he wanted to forget her. He *desperately* wanted to forget her.

But fear niggled at him—when had he let her get under his skin? When had he started to care for her?

Had he fallen in love?

God help him. No. He could not be in love with a city girl who made ten times more money than him, one who had lied to him and nearly stolen his home right out from under him.

Hell, he still wasn't sure the ranch was secure. The deal with Landon had helped, but Wallace was being a stickler about making up for the missed payments.

"Hey, cowboy, how about a dance?"

Rafe told himself to say yes. But then he looked into the redhead's pretty green eyes and thought, why bother? It wouldn't be fair to this lady to hold her in his arms when he really wanted to hold someone else.

"Sorry, darlin', but I was just leaving." Cursing himself for being even more of a fool, he threw down a few bills to cover the bar tab and limped outside for some fresh air. He should have stuck with training horses.

"DAD, YOU LOOK so much better." Suzanne hugged her father, then placed the box of chocolates on the end table, relieved to see some color had returned to his cheeks. A potted plant sat on the coffee table, a fresh flower arrangement on another end table, and other flower arrangements covered the piano.

He clasped Eleanor's hand in his and smiled. "My wife has been babying me to no end."

The comment was so unlike her father that Suzanne laughed. Worry lined Eleanor's face and the affectionate way the two were holding hands created

myriad emotions inside Suzanne: happiness for her
father that he'd finally found love again, as well as
sadness that she'd failed so horribly in her own personal life.

"I see you've been keeping the florist busy."

His father grinned, his face reddening as if
embarrassed. A cactus from her uncle Wiley. The
orange-and-yellow-striped bow should have been a
dead giveaway.

"Now, what's wrong, Suz?" her father asked.
"You don't look like yourself."

Suzanne shrugged. "Just tired, Dad. You gave us
quite a scare."

"I'm sorry." He squeezed Eleanor's hand again
and she kissed his cheek.

"I'll go make some tea for everyone." Tucking a
curl behind her ear, she hummed as she headed to
the kitchen.

"You two seem like you're getting along well,"
Suzanne said.

"That heart attack was the wake-up call your old
dad needed." He patted the space beside him on the
sofa. "Life's too short not to appreciate the nice
things in life. You have to stop and smell the roses."

Hadn't her grandmother said as much in her letter
to Suzanne? *The simple things are the best.*

Unfortunately Suzanne had realized it all too late.

"Tell me what's really bothering you now." Her
father lifted her hand in his, his eyes narrowing at
the absence of the sapphire ring James had given her.
"You turned down James's proposal?"

Suzanne nodded, uncomfortable with this tender side of her father. "Have you spoken with him?"

"Not about personal matters, but he was ecstatic over your ideas for Sugar Hill. Specialty shops and antiques and arts and crafts stores should go over well there. I can't believe I didn't think of it myself."

"Grammy Rose and Rebecca and the girls gave me the idea."

"It's brilliant. And it should make everyone in the town happy as well as boost the economy."

Suzanne nodded. "I hope so. We have a long way to go to get the project off the ground, though."

Her father tipped her chin up with his thumb. "So, why don't you look happy? Having second thoughts about James?"

"No, it's not James."

"Then who?"

Suzanne glanced at the door, hoping Eleanor would rescue her, but had no such luck.

"It's that cowboy, isn't it?" Her father sighed. "I thought there was something going on between the two of you when I saw you together."

"There is nothing going on," Suzanne said. "He hates me."

"What?" His eyebrows shot up. "How could any man hate my daughter? You're lovely and smart and—"

"And I deceived him, Dad. I went to Sugar Hill to talk him into selling his ranch, but I didn't tell him that I was working for James."

"Oh." He scratched his chin. "But you were doing your job. The man has to understand that."

"He doesn't understand why I lied. He's an honest man, Dad. And the Lazy M Ranch has been in his family for generations."

"An honest, broke man but sentimental, huh?"

"Money isn't everything."

"But you can't pay bills without it, now, can you?"

Suzanne shrugged. That was the problem. And short of paying off Rafe's loans for him, she didn't know how to help him.

She clutched her father's hand. That was it, she would find out how much he needed and make an anonymous donation. She had plenty of savings stored away that she'd planned to use to buy her condo instead of renting. And she loved Rafe enough to part with it. To save his beloved land and the memories his mother treasured. After all, life was too short; she could replace the money, but his mother's memories were irreplaceable. Mrs. McAllister would lose the tree she'd planted when he was born and the one where she and her husband had married.

This was one thing she could do for Rafe and his mother, something to make up for her lies and for hurting him.

And if she worked it right, Rafe would never have to know....

THE NEXT WEEK was one of the longest weeks in Rafe's life. Every time he turned around, his mother

was asking about Suzanne. Or he was seeing re-
minders of the woman who had glided into his life
like a fairy angel, broken his heart and disappeared
just as quickly.

Now, when he rode across the pasture and looked
at the mountains, he remembered Suzanne's look of
awe at the splendor. When he passed the falls, he
saw her nearly naked body, floating in the mist, her
smile as radiant as the moonlight skating over the icy
water.

Even Hazel and her baby calf reminded him of the
danged woman.

Unfortunately, his mother's newfound romance
with Bud emphasized the fact that he was alone, driving the nail of despair deeper into his own wounded
flesh.

He had mended every piece of broken fence he
could find, he and Bud and Red had branded the new
steers, and at night he had labored over the books,
trying to squirrel out a few extra thousand.

Thursday afternoon, he entered the bank, his head
high, praying Slim Wallace had softened on his de-
mands since Horton Developers had backed off
wanting his property. Another reminder of Suzanne.

Apparently, she was the new town hero.

He reluctantly admitted he admired her solution.
But he hadn't admired her lies.

Was she enjoying being back in Atlanta? Spending
her days with the city crowd, her nights with Horton?
The thought made his stomach sour.

The floor creaked as he stepped past the tellers to

Wallace's office. He was surprised to see Bud sitting in the man's office.

"Come on in," Wallace said.

Rafe frowned and raised his brow in question. Bud gave him a sheepish grin and cracked his knuckles.

"You want me to wait till you're done?" Rafe asked, wondering if Bud was here to borrow money. He sure as hell hadn't been able to give him a raise lately.

"No, sit down," Wallace said.

"I asked to join you," Bud explained, then cleared his throat, his gaze straying nervously.

Wallace laid a folder on his desk, then handed Rafe a copy. "All right, let's talk business."

Rafe reached in his pocket and pulled out the check he'd written earlier, hating that he'd had to accept money from Landon, but he had no choice. "This should get me almost caught up."

Wallace took the check and studied it, then dropped it on his desk.

"And this should cover the rest," Bud said, drawing out his own checkbook and scribbling out a check.

Rafe swallowed hard. "What the hell are you doing, Bud?"

"Helping out a friend," Bud said. "Actually two friends. You and your mama."

"I'm not taking your charity." Rafe shot to his feet. "Put your checkbook back in your pocket."

"Don't be stubborn, Rafe," Bud said. "You need the money, I've got it. Call it a loan if you want."

"If you've got so much money, how come you're working for me?"

Bud shrugged. "I like the Lazy M." His grin turned sheepish again. "And I've liked your mama for a long time."

Rafe stared at him dumbfounded. "But—"

"But nothing, Rafe. I want to marry your mother, so why shouldn't I contribute to the ranch, something besides sweat and hard work? I want to be more."

"Like a partner?"

"Gentlemen, this is all very touching," Wallace said wryly, "but unnecessary." He handed Bud back his check. "The loan has been paid off."

"What?" The chair skidded across the floor when Rafe stumbled backward and bumped it.

"You heard me. An anonymous donor paid you up for the next three months."

Rafe turned to Bud. "Did you do this?"

"No." Bud held up his hands. "Honest. Else why would I be here?"

Rafe grunted in frustration. "Who did it, Wallace? You have to tell me."

Wallace tugged at the collar of his shirt. "I can't rightly say, Rafe. But if I were you, I'd count my lucky stars that someone was looking out for you."

Rafe swore and stalked out, determined to find out who had done the good deed.

A good deed that he would rectify—a good deed that had humiliated him in front of Wallace and his own ranch hand.

"SUZANNE?"

Suzanne glanced up from her desk to see James approaching. Since her return to Atlanta, their relationship had been strained. She hadn't broken the man's heart, she realized when she'd heard he was dating their secretary, but she imagined she had wounded his pride.

Men and their darned egos.

The very reason she had to keep the fact that she had paid off Rafe's debts a secret. She could imagine the cowboy's reaction. Stubborn, sexy, cowboy—

"Suzanne, did you hear me?"

She startled, dragging herself back to reality. "I'm sorry, I guess I was preoccupied."

His disgusted frown irritated her. "Listen, the mayor of Sugar Hill called, and the town definitely wants our company to oversee the development."

"That's great, James."

"But they have one stipulation—they want you to run the show."

"What?"

"The mayor said he doesn't want to work with anyone but you. Something about being a Hartwell and family ties and that kind of garbage."

"It's not garbage," Suzanne said, bristling. "But he knows I'll be loyal and do the project right."

"Then you want to do it?" His incredulous tone irked her more. "It would mean living in Sugar Hill for at least six months. Maybe a year."

So close to Rafe. Could she stand it?

At least she would have her family close by. Her cousins, her sister. Here all she had was an empty

condo that meant nothing to her. And a lot of lonesome nights.

Besides, she probably wouldn't see much of Rafe,
as he didn't come into town that often.

"Call him and tell him I'll do it."

James gaped at her as if she was a fool. And
maybe she was, but in the short time she'd been in
Sugar Hill, she'd changed. She didn't want to lose
that part of herself.

Even if she never won Rafe back.

"BUD TOLD ME what happened in town today,"
Rafe's mother said over dinner.

Rafe speared the man with a cross look. "Yeah,
you got any ideas who'd do such a thing?"

"You make it sound like someone stole from us."

He slammed his fist down on the table, sending
cutlery rattling. "They treated us like a damn charity
case." If he found out it was Landon, he'd damn
well turn it down. He wouldn't make the same mis-
takes his father had. Getting indebted to the man,
then owing him and having to trade favors later.

His mother pushed her plate back and glared at
him. "Rafe McAllister, you're acting like a child.
Now, stop throwing a tantrum and be grateful."

"You know who it was, don't you?"

"No." She dotted her mouth with her napkin. "I
assumed it was Bud."

"But it wasn't," Bud said. "Although I would
like to contribute and be a part of the family."

Bud dropped to his knees. "I love you, honey. I know I'm just an old ranch hand, and I don't have my own place, but I've got money saved that I can contribute to the Lazy M. Would you consider marrying me?"

"Oh, Bud." His mother pressed her hand over her mouth, tears streaming down her cheeks.

Rafe watched in stunned silence, his chest tightening.

"Well?" Bud pressed a hand over his heart. "You're making me crazy waiting. Please say yes."

"I love you, too," his mother whispered in a shaky voice. "And I'd love to marry you." He kissed her hand, then stood. His mother stood at the same time and the two embraced, kissing and gushing over each other like teenagers.

"Congratulations," Rafe said as they pulled apart. He hugged his mother. "I'm happy for you, Mom." He shook Bud's hand. "And I can't think of anyone I'd rather have in the family."

Rafe pinched the bridge of his nose with his fingers. He'd never felt so sentimental.

Or alone.

He strode out to the barn, saddled Thunder and mounted him, then rode toward his favorite part of the ranch. His mother was getting married and he was happy for her. She was past the hurt of losing his father and was moving on with her life. The ranch was saved, temporarily, although as soon as he found out who'd paid off his debts, he would make sure he'd returned the money.

The waterfall crashed against the icy rocks, splashing and rippling with a gusto that mocked his own bad mood. He could see Suzanne standing beneath the water, her dark hair cascading down past her shoulders, her head thrown back in the throes of laughter and passion. He itched to reach out, to touch her again, to make the moment real. To have her in his arms one more time.

But he would go home alone tonight. And every night after.

For the first time in his life he wanted something more than his land. More than the ranch and raising cattle and breaking horses.

He wanted Suzanne. In spite of what she'd done to him, he still wanted her. And not just in his bed, though he craved that with every ounce of his being.

No, this was much worse. He wanted her as his wife.

Chapter Seventeen

Suzanne had spent a long, sleepless night thinking about Rafe and wishing things had turned out differently. Now she'd joined her cousins and Rebecca for their weekly night out, but her heart wasn't in it. She would never be happily married like them.

Because her heart belonged to a man who didn't love her.

"What's up?" Mimi gestured toward Alison's plate. "You're not eating very much."

Alison grinned sheepishly. "Well, I was going to wait until Brady and I were together to tell you but—"

"You're pregnant!" Mimi shouted.

Rebecca suddenly started coughing as if she were choking on her water, and all eyes turned toward her.

"Oh, my goodness, so are you," Suzanne said. "Aren't you, Bec?"

Rebecca nodded. "I...I just took a test this morning."

Chaos erupted with all the girls crying and shouting and hugging at once.

"This is unbelievable," Hannah said, covering her full stomach with her hand. "Maggie Rose is going to have a new cousin anyday now. And the two of you are right behind."

Tears stung Suzanne's eyes. "It's wonderful. I'm so happy for all of you."

A quiet rippled through them.

"I really am," Suzanne said, realizing she sounded emotional and hating it. Maybe the old Suzanne was better, the heartless businesswoman who wanted or needed no one.

The girl she'd been before meeting Rafe and falling in love.

Rebecca squeezed her arm. "Things aren't working out for you and Rafe?"

Suzanne shook her head. "I don't want to talk about him." She fidgeted with her napkin, pasting on a smile. "And I certainly don't want to put a damper on all this exciting news. How are you two feeling?" She clasped Rebecca's hand and glanced at Alison.

"I'm great," Alison said. "Just a little queasy in the morning."

"Me, too. But as long as I eat every two hours, I'm fine," Rebecca said. "I'll probably gain a million pounds."

The girls laughed. "We'll keep a watch on it," Hannah assured her.

"Just think, Hannah can deliver all the Hartwell

babies," Alison said. "It's so nice having a doctor in the family."

"Yes, we admire you," Suzanne said.

"Me? Hey, you're the genius," Hannah said. "Finding a way to satisfy everyone in town and help the community took talent."

"We were all impressed," Alison added.

Mimi sipped her lemonade. "Everyone in town is talking about how smart you are. They can't wait to get started on the flea market idea."

"I'm glad," Suzanne said. "I'm sure there are a lot of creative people here in Sugar Hill."

"Don't you know it." Mimi beamed. "Mr. Zimmerman is a glass blower, three of the ladies from church have already organized the quilting circle, Roger Gunthrie has metal-art projects coming out of his ears and Paula Putts wants to start a consignment shop."

"That should go over really well," Rebecca said.

"And you're going to show your paintings, aren't you?" Alison asked Rebecca.

Rebecca blushed. "Yes, I guess so."

"Of course you are," Hannah said. "After the murals you painted for the clinic, the committee for the flea market will probably want you to decorate their booths."

The girls gushed over ideas for several minutes, everything ranging from historic scenes of the towns and mountains beyond to bright borders of teddy bears for a children's clothing booth to a ranch scene for the Western wear Waldo Turner wanted to sell.

Boots and hats—Suzanne couldn't help but think of Rafe and his ranch, how sexy he looked in that Stetson. How she'd like to make love to him again wearing nothing but that Stetson.

How she would never have a little baby for Hannah to deliver because the only man's baby she wanted was Rafe's.

"Earth to Suzanne," Mimi said, waving her hands. "You zoned out on us."

"I know you said you don't want to talk about it, but please tell us what's going on with Rafe," Alison said softly.

"It might help to talk about it," Rebecca said sympathetically.

"Did you try the belly dancing?" Mimi asked.

Suzanne shook her head and frowned into her coffee, her appetite nonexistent. "He found out that I worked for James and he despises me. It was awful," she admitted. "Then James came in and announced he was my fiancé."

"But he's not, is he?" Rebecca asked in horror.

"No, I broke that off later. But not until the morning after Dad's heart attack. I was going to call James the night before, then we had to go to the hospital and…it just all happened so fast."

Rebecca patted her hand. "Well, we'll think of something."

"Go talk to him," Alison said.

Hannah rubbed her back. "Yeah, if he's the one, don't let him get away."

''Do whatever it takes,'' Mimi said. ''Even if you have to seduce the heck out of him.''

Suzanne studied her cousins' and sister's faces. They were right. If this had been a business deal, she wouldn't accept defeat so easily. She'd be prepared to go to war to win. Getting the man of her dreams would be no different.

''All right. I will.''

''You'll seduce him?'' Mimi asked.

Suzanne grinned and waved the waitress over to order some nonalcoholic champagne to celebrate the pregnancies, and two glasses of real wine for her and Mimi. ''I'll do whatever it takes.'' After all, she already had the cowboy bridal hat, choker and boots.

Now all she needed was for Cupid to perform a miracle, and she would be wearing them at her own wedding.

RAFE COULDN'T BELIEVE his mother and Bud were already planning their wedding.

Their excitement filled the once-quiet house, while he had to force himself not to be an ogre because he wanted to be in the groom's shoes. For once. He couldn't figure out why. He had never wanted marriage or a family before—not until Suzanne.

Which only proved how well Suzanne's trap had worked and what a fool he had been to fall for her. But he would disentangle himself, he had to.

Time would help, he promised himself. One day at a time and the memories would slip away until they would be nothing more than a distant dot of nothingness in his brain.

At least, he hoped that was what happened.

Unfortunately, so far the ache in his chest just seemed to feel worse and worse.

As soon as he entered the house, he heard his mother humming some sappy song about love being in the air. She had discarded the walker a week ago, too, and had a little bounce to her step.

Just as he'd finished washing off the worst of the dust from his hands and face, a knock sounded at the door. He hesitated, wondering who had decided to pay them a visit. Maybe one of his mother's friends, who'd dropped by to help her plan the wedding.

Feeling surly, he strode to the door, surprised to find Suzanne's father, Bert, standing on the other side of the screen. "Dr. Hartwell?"

"Yes. Can I come in?"

Rafe finished drying his hands on the hand towel and opened the door. "Certainly, sir. Rafe McAllister." He extended his hand, wondering what the hell the man had in mind. Did he know Rafe had slept with his daughter? Was something wrong with Suzanne? His heart pounded. "How are you feeling?"

"Nice to meet you, McAllister." He patted his chest self-consciously. "And the ticker's just fine. My daughter's told me a lot about you." He shifted, his gaze taking in Rafe's humble house. "Er, I mean about your ranch."

Rafe nodded. So, had she sent her father here in

another attempt to get him to sell? "I thought Horton Developers had decided they didn't want my land?"

Hartwell wrinkled his forehead in a frown. "That's correct."

"Then I don't understand why you're here, sir."

Another, deeper frown. "I...thought we should talk." He gestured toward the den. "Can we sit down for a minute?"

"Sure." Rafe was truly puzzled, but he hadn't meant to be rude. "Come on in." He led the way to the den, forcing himself not to apologize for the old-fashioned couch and furnishings. His mother liked antiques, didn't have the money for fancy stuff like this man was probably used to.

Another reminder he and Suzanne had been wrong for each other.

Suzanne's father took a seat in the wing chair and stretched out his legs, then propped his elbows on his knees and steepled his hands. "I came to offer you a business deal."

Rafe simply stared at him, perplexed. "What kind of business deal?"

"Actually, I understand your ranch needs some extra funding and I'm proposing a loan of sorts."

Red-hot humiliation flooded Rafe. Had Suzanne shared his financial situation with her father?

"I don't follow," he said. "Why would you do that?"

Hartwell shrugged. "My daughter seems to think you're worth it."

Rafe clamped his hands by his side to control his

temper. "She asked you to come here and offer me money?"

"No, she has no idea I'm here. But I understand you have a lot of land, a decent herd from what I've been told, and I'm always looking to invest."

"Exactly what would you get in exchange for this loan?" He wasn't trying to buy him, was he?

"Like I said, it would be an investment. We can work out the terms for repayment. With interest, of course."

Rafe had heard enough. He stood, signifying the meeting was over. "I appreciate your offer, Dr. Hartwell, but I can't accept it." He was amazed at how calm his voice sounded when he was seething inside like a volcano about to blow.

"Don't be a fool, son. You need the money."

"Actually, I don't need it right now, sir. But like I said, thanks for your charitable offer."

Hartwell winced at the emphasis he'd placed on the word *charitable,* and Rafe knew he'd gotten the message. But the man's offer planted another seed of wonder in Rafe's mind.

The anonymous donor, the person who'd paid his debt—he'd thought it had to be his mother, that maybe she'd had some money in savings, or that Wallace had decided to cut him a break. But now he had a feeling he'd been wrong. He knew who had paid his debts. He refused to sit back and let it stand.

He'd promised himself he wasn't going to see Suzanne again, but now he would have to.

And he'd tell her to take her money and get the hell out of his life.

SUZANNE HAD TRIED to make the chocolate cake again, but this time it looked more like a crater than a cake, so she ditched it and stopped by Mimi's coffee shop once again. Armed with the dessert and a book of new crocheting patterns she had found in Rebecca's bookstore, she sped toward the Lazy M, hoping her peace offerings would at least get her through the front door.

She had to force Rafe to listen to her, make him understand how much she cared for him.

Starting with his mother might be a cheap shot, but she really loved the older woman and missed her, and she *was* desperate.

Dusk painted the ranch with its heavenly glow, the blue sky above a menagerie of orange and gold and red. She remembered riding across the land with Rafe and seeing the beautiful mountains, the waterfall, the pride in his smile as he showed her his spread, and her heart squeezed.

Parking in front of the farmhouse, she gathered the cake and book, struggling not to fall as her foot skidded on the loose gravel. She should have worn flats, but she'd taken Mimi's advice and worn the short black skirt, scooped blue top and heels to showcase her body. Shameless but effective, Mimi had said. Suzanne hoped she was right.

Juggling the cake and book into one hand, she knocked, her breath rasping with nerves. Seconds later the door swung open and Mrs. McAllister greeted her with a hug. "It's so nice to see you, darlin', come on in."

Suzanne smiled, the woman's warm loving embrace acting like a balm to her aching heart. She hadn't realized how much she'd missed having a mother until she'd befriended the elderly woman.

"You look great," Suzanne said, noticing the absence of the walker and the color in Mrs. McAllister's cheeks.

"I feel great," Rafe's mother said. "Guess what, dear? I'm getting married."

"Married?"

"Yes!" Mrs. McAllister ushered her in. "Come on in, and I'll tell you all about it." She spied the gifts in Suzanne's arms. "Aren't you sweet? I'll get Maria to make us some coffee and I'll fill you in on the wedding plans."

Suzanne laughed at her exuberance and followed her to the den. A few minutes later they shared the cake and coffee while Mrs. McAllister ranted about her newfound love with Bud.

"I'm so happy for you," Suzanne said.

"And I'm happy for you. I hear you're going to oversee the new development. I'm very proud of you, Suzanne."

Pride and happiness swelled inside her chest, along with guilt. She had to tell this sweet woman the truth. So she spilled the beans, everything from how she'd come here to meet Rafe and had deceived him, to

how she had changed her mind once she'd spent time
on the ranch.

"Well, dear, no wonder my son has been acting
so ornery lately."

"I...don't blame him for despising me," Suzanne
said. "But I want to apologize and talk to him—"

"What are you doing here?" Rafe's husky voice
cut into the room like thunder.

Suzanne jumped, nearly knocking her coffee cup
off the table. Rafe's mother twisted toward him with
a chastising, motherly look.

"She's visiting me," Mrs. McAllister said. "And
we've had a lovely chat. You should hear her out,
too."

Rafe scowled at her. "I'm not interested in anything she has to say. In fact, I just came from your
apartment." He glared at Suzanne. "I wanted to give
you back this." He dropped a check in her lap, a
muscle in his jaw ticking. "I don't accept charity."

"What are you talking about, son?"

"The anonymous donor who paid off my loan. I
thought for sure it was you or Wallace or even Landon, that he would call in his marker sometime, but
it seems Ms. Hartwell did. Trying to buy your way
back into our lives, Suzanne?"

The air left Suzanne's lungs in a painful rush as
if someone had kicked her in the chest. Tears welled
up in her eyes, and her hands began to shake. But
beneath the pain her temper surfaced.

"Rafe McAllister, how dare you talk to our guest

like that!'' Mrs. McAllister stood, her eyes dark with displeasure.

''Our guest can take her charity and go back to Atlanta where she belongs. We don't need or want her here anymore.''

Rafe turned on his heels and charged out the door. Suzanne heard the door slam behind him and bit back a sob.

Mrs. McAllister pressed a hand on Suzanne's shoulder. ''I'm sorry for my boy's bad manners, but he has a lot of stubborn pride, just like his daddy.''

''I...know. That's one of the things I love about him.''

Mrs. McAllister took Suzanne's hands in hers. ''If you really love him, then make him listen.''

Suzanne looked into the wise woman's eyes and nodded. Her determination back in place, she kissed Mrs. McAllister's cheek, then went to tell Rafe exactly how she felt about him.

And he would listen, even if she had to hog-tie him in the barn to keep him from escaping.

Chapter Eighteen

Rafe hated the way he'd caused a scene in front of his mother, but he seemed to have no control over himself whenever he was around Suzanne. And to think that she had sat in his house with his own mother, acting all chummy. The sight had thrown him for a loop and made him want to grab her and kiss her.

In fact, the only way he could keep his hands off her was to remember his anger and the humiliation she had caused him.

He grabbed the shovel to muck the stalls when footsteps sounded behind him.

"Rafe McAllister, I know you're mad," she said, "but you're going to listen to me."

"Look, I've had just about enough of you Hart-wells offering me charity." He almost spat into the dust. "By the way, thanks for telling your father about my financial situation. That was real decent of you."

"My father?" Her mouth gaped open.

If he hadn't known better, he would have thought she was truly shocked. But he'd been sure her father had been lying, that she had put him up to coming. "Yes, he paid me a little visit to offer me a loan, but I turned him down just like I am you."

"Oh, my gosh, Rafe, I had no idea."

He swung around. The image of her all fired up, her dark hair tangled around the angry flush of her cheeks, her hands on those luscious hips, nearly made his knees buckle. She was so damn sexy he wanted to have his way with her right there in the hay.

He clenched his jaw instead and leaned on the shovel like a crutch.

"I swear I didn't know Dad came by. He must have known I was worried about you and he was trying to help."

"I don't need or want your help. What kind of man do you take me for?"

"I think you're strong and resourceful and handsome and full of too much stubborn pride."

He fumed at her. What was she doing, giving him compliments and insults at the same time?

She crossed the barn in three strides and yanked the shovel from his hand. "But I said you're going to listen and you damn well are. Now, I understand you have reason to be mad, and I was wrong not to tell you that I worked for Horton Developers when I first met you. And I should have told you about James. His proposal had come as a shock to him. At the time, I had no idea how I was going to answer him.''

"Because you're in love with him?" Rafe snarled, the green-eyed monster of jealousy clawing at him.

She held up a hand. "That didn't come out right. What I meant to say was that I…I actually considered his proposal but only because at the time, I had no idea what real love was. His offer was more of a business proposition than a marriage proposal.''

"I see.'' Actually, he didn't, but he refused to hear any more about the other man. "Your life is always about business, isn't it?''

"It used to be,'' she said in a voice tinged with emotion. "But not anymore.''

He waited, a heartbeat of silence passing, filled with tension.

"You knew when I came here that I was in favor of the big development. That's the reason you challenged me to come out and see your property—''

"Oh, so now this is my fault?''

"Let me finish,'' Suzanne said between clenched teeth.

Her temper didn't surprise him, instead it roused him even more. Damn it, how could he still be attracted to her when she'd lied to him?

"When you challenged me,'' she said, her voice growing softer, "I was certain I would sway you into believing it was better for you to sell, Rafe. You needed the money, and Horton Developers needed your land. I really thought the deal would be lucrative for all of us. But…'' She hesitated and fiddled

with her hair, drawing his gaze to the long column
of her neck, eliciting fantasies about kissing her
again. Oblivious to his turmoil, she continued, "But
instead I saw your side, that you were right."

He chewed the inside of his cheek. What had she
just said?

"I saw the beauty of the land and how much you
loved it and how much your mother treasured her
memories. I realized that no amount of money could
ever replace what you have here. You have a real
home, something I never had."

He swallowed, his emotions flying into a tailspin.
Admiration rose for her, unexpected and just as unwanted. Not many people would admit they were
wrong, and it took guts for her to do so. She almost
sounded wistful, envious of his humble house.

She licked her lips. "I considered telling you that
I worked for Horton Developers a while back, but I
decided to look for alternative sites for the development first."

"Really?"

"Yes." She walked toward him, but he stiffened,
and she froze, circling her arms around her waist.

"And then things got hot between us, and—"

"You were still wearing Horton's ring?"

She winced, regret shadowing her face. "Yes,
right before Dad's heart attack I decided to tell James
that I couldn't marry him. Then my dad collapsed,
and I was so upset and we wound up together,
and...well, everything just happened so fast I didn't
have a chance."

He wanted to believe her. Desperately wanted to touch her.

But she had hurt him, had humiliated him by paying off his loan.

"Why did you come here, Suzanne?"

Her gaze met his, hunger and need and remorse filling her lovely eyes. "Because I care about you, Rafe."

"Is that the reason you paid off my debts? Pity?"

"It wasn't pity," she said, her voice tight with renewed anger. "It was because I love you, Rafe. I love you and I wanted to make everything up to you. I didn't want you to lose your home."

His throat felt so thick he couldn't swallow. She couldn't mean what she'd just said.

And even if she did, didn't she realize that she had stomped on his pride? That he couldn't accept her money, that he would always feel as if she'd bought him, that she didn't respect him because he couldn't take care of her?

That he had nothing to offer her.

The tension crackled between them, the sound of the farm animals, the horses neighing outside, floating into the quiet. Even amidst the hay and stench of horse dung, she looked breathtakingly beautiful. And he would forever remember those three little words she'd just murmured.

"I...I don't know what else to say except that I'm sorry, Rafe. I'm sorry and I love you."

Then she turned and left the barn, the scent of her

perfume lingering long after he heard her car disappear into the night.

SUZANNE LET HERSELF into Rebecca's, her heart shattering. This was her apartment now. She'd officially let her lease go on her condo in Atlanta, so she could pay rent here while she oversaw the new development. She would have to make it her home. She certainly wouldn't be making a home with Rafe.

At least she had tried. Short of begging, she had done everything she could to convince Rafe she was sorry. And she had been brutally honest, even when she'd confessed her love.

But he hadn't returned the words or feelings.

Because he didn't love her.

Just like the other men in her past.

She headed to the bedroom to change into her nightgown when she spotted the hope chest. The cowgirl bridal hat and boots. She picked them up, one at a time, tracing a finger over the lacy edges, then slipped them back inside the chest. How ironic that she'd laughed when she'd first seen them, and now all she could do was cry.

IT GALLED RAFE that he had to accept Bud's money, but he'd rather take the loan from him than Suzanne. "I'll pay you back, man, as soon as we sell some of the heifers." He still didn't understand why he'd had no calls about boarders.

"I don't want you to pay me back," Bud said. "Consider it my contribution to the family."

"You don't need—"

"Yes, I do," Bud said. "I have my pride, too, Rafe. I'm not going to freeload off you and your mother."

Rafe's hand tightened around the check. He hadn't meant to insult Bud. And although he'd always thought of him as a ranch hand, he realized Bud had been a friend for years, practically a member of the family. Maybe they should make it official; he could let him buy into part of the ranch. "I didn't mean to imply you were, Bud."

"Then say no more about it." Bud chewed a blade of grass between his teeth. "You are a damn fool to let Miss Suzanne go. A stubborn damn fool."

"I don't recall asking you." Rafe turned to brush down the horses.

"You didn't. But I had to say it." Bud scratched his chin. "When your daddy was alive, I sat back and watched him cheat on your mama and I never said a word. Stupidest thing I ever did."

"It's not the same thing, Bud."

"In a way it is. I didn't think I had anything to offer your mama back then. Thought if I didn't have my own spread or a lot of money I wasn't worthy of her."

Rafe's hand stilled on the saddle.

"Is that what you think now, boy? That I'm not worthy of her, that I want to mooch off your mama?"

Worry roughened the older man's voice. Rafe shook his head. "No, Bud, of course not. You're the best thing that's happened to my mother in a long time."

Bud studied him for a long minute, obviously trying to decide if Rafe was sincere. "That's 'cause I care for her," Bud said in a thick voice. "Money ain't the most important thing in the world, you know. It's family, and family works together, during the good times and the bad."

Rafe glared at the older man. "I never said money was the most important thing."

Bud chuckled sardonically. "Hell, yeah, that's exactly what you did when you threw Miss Suzanne's check back in her face."

Rafe stared at his friend as he loped off and shook his head. That wasn't the way it had gone down at all.

Was it?

THREE DAYS LATER, Suzanne fought a wave of dizziness as she finished reviewing the plans the mayor had dropped off. She had to start eating right again, but her appetite had been nonexistent the past few days. Not since she'd declared her love to Rafe and realized that he didn't return it.

Grabbing a handful of saltines to ward off the nausea that had threatened since five this morning, she headed to the shower to dress for Mrs. McAllister's wedding, reminding herself that she didn't have to talk to Rafe. But she had promised the kind woman she'd attend, and she wouldn't disappoint her for anything in the world.

Not even if Rafe didn't want her there.

Thirty minutes later she dressed in a baby-blue silk sleeveless dress, adding pearl studs to her ears as she studied the cross her mother had given her in the mirror. She had bought one for Rafe's mother, as a wedding present and a show of friendship, and had wrapped it in silver paper. Somehow she knew her mother would approve if she were still alive. She and Mrs. McAllister might have even been friends.

Slipping on beige sandals, she brushed a little blush on her cheeks to hide her pale color and added a touch of lipstick. Then she grabbed the gift, sucked up her courage and headed to her car. She hoped the wedding didn't last too long.

Every minute in Rafe's presence would be torture.

RAFE'S BREATH CAUGHT in his throat at the sight of his mother on his arm. She and Bud had decided to marry beside the waterfall on the property. The place where he had fallen for Suzanne.

She wore a simple off-white lace dress with a hat, the smile on her face radiant. ''You look beautiful, Mom.''

''Thank you, honey.'' She adjusted his navy-blue tie. ''You look pretty swanky yourself.''

He chuckled. ''Yeah, well, this monkey suit's coming off as soon as the ceremony is over.''

She laughed and looped her arm through his. ''Can we talk for a minute?''

''Sure. Is something wrong? Because if you're having second thoughts—''

"I'm not having second thoughts. But I was hoping *you* were about Suzanne."

"Mom—"

"Listen, Rafe, I appreciate the fact that you've tried to protect me the past few months, that you didn't want me to know the extent of our debt, and you tried to keep your father's gambling and affair from me…"

Shock rode through him.

"But I knew all along."

"You did?" He couldn't believe it. "Then why didn't you say something?"

She smiled sadly. "Because I knew it would upset you. Now I'm thinking I was wrong. I loved your father, but he wasn't a perfect man. In fact, I loved him enough to forgive him."

"But he hurt you—"

"Yes, he did. But he only slipped up that one time, and he tried to quit gambling." She cleared her throat, swiped at a tear. "What I'm saying here is that love is about forgiveness and acceptance and working together. If the old coot hadn't been so stubborn and had let me work like I offered, we might not have gotten so deeply in debt."

He studied her face, letting her words sink in. His mother had wanted to work to help out, but his father had refused. He had been stubborn and prideful, and it had almost cost him the Lazy M.

But Landon had said his father had had lots of women. Had his mother been in the dark about them, or had Landon lied? And if he had lied about that, could he have lied about other things—like how much money his father owed him?

"It's always easier to give love than it is to accept it," his mother said softly as she kissed him on the cheek. "But it's important to be able to do both."

"It's time," Maria yelled. "The wedding march is beginning, *señora.*"

Red, who'd offered to play the guitar, began strumming the wedding march. He walked her across the grassy bank, spotting several of his mother's friends sitting in the fold-up chairs near the falls, Suzanne wedged in between two of the elderly women.

Suddenly his mother's words and Bud's advice sank into his brain. His very stubborn, prideful brain.

Nothing really mattered except the fact that he was in love with Suzanne. And that she loved him.

Did she still love him?

"Dearly beloved, we are gathered here today..." the preacher began.

Rafe barely heard the words as his mother and Bud exchanged vows. He couldn't take his eyes off Suzanne. Their gazes locked, the ceremony fading into a distant haze.

He remembered Suzanne challenging him at the town meeting that day, then climbing on Blondie for the first time. He saw her standing in the falls with him, tossing off her clothes, water cascading down her slender back. He saw her lying naked in his arms, kissing and stroking his body until he came apart. He saw the tears glistening in her eyes when he'd returned her mother's necklace, then again when he'd thrown her unselfish offer of money in her face.

He heard her saying she loved him.

But he had never said the words back.

She possessed far more courage than he did. His chest squeezed as he realized that he had hurt her.

He would spend the rest of his life making up for it.

"I now pronounce you husband and wife," the preacher said. Bud took his mother in his arms and they kissed, the chorus of oohs and aahs evaporating into a fog around Rafe as he walked toward Suzanne.

Then Rafe was cutting through the crowd of well-wishers, holding out his hand and dragging her to the side.

"Suzanne—"

"Rafe."

"No, let me," he said in a voice thick with emotion. Without taking his eyes off her, he cupped her face in his hands. "I'm sorry I've been so…so difficult. I'm sorry I sent you away. I'm sorry I didn't call." He hesitated, then dropped to his knees in the grass. "But I know now that I love you, Suzanne. And if you'll have me, I want to marry you."

Her lower lip trembled, and for a heartbeat he waited, expecting her to launch herself into his arms. But she didn't. She shook her head, a single tear sliding down her cheek.

"I can't, Rafe."

"What?"

"Not if you won't accept my help." She swiped

at her eyes, and he understood what the tears cost her. "I want a real marriage, where we work together, Rafe, where—"

"Shh." He stood and dragged her into his arms and kissed her. When he pulled back, he was shaking. "We'll work all that out. It may take me a while to get the hang of a relationship, but we'll work together."

"You're sure?"

"Yes, I don't need your money for the loan right now, but if you want to use your money to buy some furniture for the house, that's fine. I want you to fix it up so it'll be your home, so you'll be happy there."

She threaded her fingers in his hair. "Rafe, don't you understand? All I need to be happy is you."

He gripped her arms in his hands. Now that he'd touched her again, he couldn't stand to let her go. "Then say you'll marry me," he whispered roughly, still not satisfied without the words.

"Yes, I'll marry you."

"I love you, Suzanne."

"I love you, too."

He swept her into his arms and kissed her with all the passion and hunger he had been holding inside. When they finally opened their eyes, the crowd of spectators had turned to watch them. "We could get married right here and now," he said, grinning at his mother who was smiling, cuddled inside her new husband's embrace.

Suzanne shook her head. "No, I want Alison to help plan my wedding, and my sister and father and

Grammy Rose to be here. Family is the most important thing in the world.'' She nuzzled his neck.

''You're right, and I want to have one with you, Suzanne.''

''I want that, too.'' She kissed his ear. ''In fact, I can't wait to get married.''

''Then you want a big church wedding?''

She shook her head. ''No, I want a cowboy wedding.'' Her fingers traced a path over his chest. ''And I'm going to be a cowgirl bride.''

Epilogue

Six Weeks Later

Her wedding couldn't have been more perfect, Suzanne thought, as she rode across her grandmother's lawn to meet Rafe on horseback. He and Bud had used his trailer to bring Thunder and Blondie up, and she wore the white bridal hat, lacy boots and choker from her hope chest, along with a tea-length cowgirl bridal gown Alison had helped her find. It matched the earring set and the beads trimming her veil. Rafe wore black dress jeans and a long black Western frock coat over a brocade striped-satin vest with a black bow tie, an outfit that made him look rakish, like a movie star. He'd traded his everyday Stetson for a new black one, his work boots for black alligator cowboy boots with silver spurs.

Her entire family had shown up for the service. Everyone was in such a festive mood with talk of Alison's and Rebecca's pregnancies. Hannah had given birth to a baby boy the week before, a strapping seven pounder with dark hair like his father's and a smile like his mother's. They named him Clint Wiley Tippins. Her uncle Wiley was ecstatic to finally have a male in the family, especially a namesake. Jake had already bought out the sporting goods store, everything from footballs to soccer balls were scattered across the infant's room.

Red roses draped the trellis on top of Pine Mountain, and she and Rafe met in front of the gazebo. He dismounted, then offered her a hand down. Together they walked into the gazebo, a symbol of the way they planned to spend the rest of their lives.

Red strummed the last chord on the guitar, and the preacher began the service.

"Who gives this woman to marry this man?"

Her father stepped forward and kissed her cheek. "Her sister and I." He gave Rafe a warning look. "You'd better be good to her."

A rumble of laughter sounded, and Rafe nodded. "Yes, sir, I intend to."

They joined hands, each reciting vows they'd written themselves.

Suzanne pressed a kiss to Rafe's hand. "Rafe, I went to Sugar Hill to start a business venture, instead, I found you and started my life. Before you, I had only emptiness and the hope of money to make me happy. But your love is much more valuable. You are my life, Rafe. I fell in love with you the first time you held me in your arms on the dance floor, and I almost lost you because of lies. From this day forward, there will be no secrets between us, only the bond of our love and the joining of our hearts forevermore.''

Rafe kissed the palm of her hand, then squeezed it between them. ''Before you came into my life, Suzanne, I thought I had everything I needed. My land, my family, the legacy of my past. But when I met you, I realized that my life wasn't complete, that my legacy lies in being with you. I was afraid to love before, now I'm afraid not to. I promise to love, honor and cherish you all the days of our lives.''

''You have rings?''

Suzanne bit her lip, praying Rafe was okay with the fact that she'd insisted on using her grandmother's simple wedding band. He smiled and slid it on her finger.

''Sometimes simple things are the best,'' she had told him.

And he had agreed.

The preacher uttered a prayer, then pronounced them husband and wife. Rafe dragged her into his arms and kissed her, the love and passion in his embrace so sweet and tender that tears flooded Suzanne's eyes.

They broke apart to applause and laughter, the chatter of their family around them filled with congratulations. Alison had arranged for a groom's cake made in the shape of a horseshoe, the Western cake topper and a charm bridal serving set completing the Western theme.

After she'd hugged all her family, Rafe's mother approached her. "I feel like I'm getting a daughter!"

Suzanne returned the hug. "And I'm getting a mom. Finally. And a wonderful home."

"It *will* be wonderful when we make a few changes," Rafe said.

Mrs. McAllister pulled back. "Rafe told you he discovered Landon had cheated his father. He's reimbursing us with all the money he owes us."

"Yeah, once something Mom said kicked in, I figured if he'd lied about one thing, he'd lied about others. I talked to Palo and he did a little checking for me, found records that showed Dad didn't owe him nearly as much as he'd claimed. Finally the Lazy M will be out of the red," Rafe added.

"That's great," Suzanne exclaimed.

"And Palo's bringing all his horses back to board as well," Rafe said. "Apparently Landon had been bad talking me around town so no one wanted to board with me."

"All that's going to change now," Mrs. McAllister said. "Landon ruined his own reputation."

Suzanne rubbed her hand along her husband's back. "I'm so glad things are working out for the McAllisters."

Rafe pulled her into his arms. "Yeah, I'd say things are definitely looking up for the McAllisters. Maybe because we learned to work together."

"Rafe," his mother said, "Bud and I have decided to move into the carriage house. We plan to fix it up for the two of us."

"Mom, you don't have to do that," Rafe said. "Suzanne and I are fine with all of us sharing the big farmhouse."

"Oh, pshaw," his mother slapped his hand and cuddled up to Bud with a grin. "We need our privacy. Besides, that house is meant for a big family. I do hope you're going to give me some grand-babies."

Suzanne blushed. She'd actually hoped she was pregnant and thought her dizzy spells earlier in the week might be a sign. She was surprised at how disappointed she'd felt when she'd realized she wasn't.

The music started up, a country band Grammy Rose had found, and everyone gathered food and began to dance. Rafe led her to the dance floor, hugging her in his arms as they swayed to the music.

"I love you so much, Mrs. McAllister."

She wrapped her arm around his neck. "And I love you, Rafe. Forever and always."

"No more secrets, right?"

She laughed, then bit down on her lip. "Well, there are a couple of things I should tell you."

"Uh-oh, like what?"

"Well, I'm not very good at gardening."

He chuckled, his body brushing hers seductively. "Honey, I figured that out the first time I saw you pulling weeds."

"Oh." She didn't realize she'd been so obvious. "And I can't sew worth a flip."

"Really?" He frowned.

"And...uh, I can't cook."

He arched a brow. "That delicious cake?"

"Compliments of Mimi's shop."

His dark eyes pierced her. "Hmm, you might have to make up for all that."

She angled her head to peer up at him. "Excuse me?"

He grinned. "I always did like that prickly spine of yours."

She laughed and curled deeper into his arms. "So, what do I have to do? Grovel? Shovel horse manure to earn my keep."

"Hmm, that'd be an idea."

"In your dreams, cowboy."

His laughter rumbled from deep in his chest. "Actually, I had something else in mind."

Suzanne pretended to give it some thought. "Does it involve kissing?"

"Oh, yeah, lots of kissing, and other indoor sports...."

She licked her lips, a slow smile spreading across her mouth. "Well, you did promise to teach me everything I needed to know about riding, cowboy."

His finger traced a gentle path down her cheek, and her breath caught. "I can't tell you how happy you've made me, Suzanne. But you've given me so much—what can I possibly give you?"

Suzanne leaned on tiptoe and whispered in his ear.
"A baby."

Rafe's look of surprise came swiftly, then he
halted and picked her up and swung her into his
arms. "How long do we have to stay at this recep-
tion, anyway?"

* * * * *

Be sure to look for Rita Herron's next book,
A Warrior's Mission
*book four in the Colorado Confidential series,
available only from Harlequin Intrigue in
December 2003.*

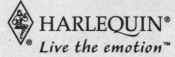

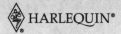

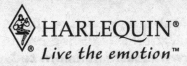

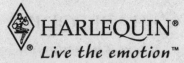